PLANET OF LOVE

A Brent and Edward Novella of the Future

The sequel to

Love Beyond Orbit

Richard Jeffery Wagner, PhD

AuctusPublishers.com

Eight minutes of grace, of light, to the planet of love
——Thomas Pynchon, ***Gravity's Rainbow***, the time it takes
a photon to travel to Earth from the sun.

I dedicate this book to my muse, Andrea, without whom none
of my books would have been possible.

Contents

Introduction

In the twenty-first century, the robot will take the place which slave labor occupied in ancient civilization.

—Nicola Tesla

This book is the fourth in the Brent and Edward series of future fiction. The first book, *The Zombie Philosopher*, introduced Brent, a philosophizing robot, and Edward Collier, a bachelor software engineer. The second book, *Brent and Edward go to Mars*, introduced Cindy Fairfax, an undercover agent investigating crime on Mars. The third book, *Love Beyond Orbit*, continued the love affair of Edward and Cindy in that paradise called Hawai'i. In this book, Brent and Edward have returned from their winter Hawaiian holiday to their home in North America. Cindy has returned to Britain for one final undercover assignment before she and Edward wed, and robotic valet Brent falls in love with the robotic maid across the road.

My stories set in the future are in the category of *hard* science fiction. That is, nothing described violates the laws of physics, and no new "science" is invented to advance the plot. In *The Zombie Philosopher*, Edward's tennis buddy Joe, an engineer who loves to talk about technology, explains fully to an assembled dinner party exactly how liquid hydrogen powered flying cars work. In *Love Beyond Orbit*, single stage ballistic rockets are the realistic norm for passenger travel with a floating spaceport offshore of Honolulu.

A dystopian future in science fiction can suggest to us what to avoid in policy, goals, social conventions, and so on. Utopian fiction, however, to the extent that it has plausible credibility, can be a positive attractor, showing us what to work toward. I described the details of that credibility in my preceding three books. First, the technological aspects of a post-scarcity economy, particularly the water economy in space based on practical nuclear fusion power sources combined with intelligent automation; secondly, the political realization of fair wealth distribution as human labor becomes less and less necessary; and finally, the abolition of war after the institution of a solar system democracy.

This book does not dwell on the utopian features of a future solar system civilization—they provide the setting for a love story. I hope you enjoy it.

Home from Hawai'i

I have learned to use the word 'impossible' with the greatest caution.

—Wernher von Braun

The ballistic passenger rocket, in freefall, arcing high over the Pacific Ocean, rotated on a horizontal axis so that the motor end would aim in the direction of eastern travel. Passengers saw the limb of the Earth rotate in the round windows, the sun, not visible, high overhead. The autopilot announced, "Acceleration in one minute." Edward Collier and Brent, his robotic valet and companion, checked their seat belts.

"That was a smooth rotation," said Edward.

"Indeed, sir, it was."

The 20-minute rocket flight from Hawai'i to the continent would be ending with two gees of thrust tapering off to one gee for a soft tail-sitting landing at Nā Hōkū Spaceport near the big city, 175 kilometers from their rural home. Edward had arranged for his flying car, Maxine, to be waiting for them at the spaceport.

Edward was still wearing his aloha shirt, but he had the foresight to put on long pants, shoes, and socks. It was mid-afternoon at the spaceport due to the time zone change. The air temperature was ten degrees Celsius as they exited the spaceport and walked to meet Maxine in the aircar landing area on this clear but breezy late-winter day. As Brent and Edward approached her,

Maxine, engines idling, opened her doors and boot lid. Brent and Edward put their luggage in the boot, got in, and Maxine closed her doors. She revved up her twin counterrotating hydrogen turbines and shot upward at one-and-a-half gees to cruising altitude and swift forward speed. "Welcome back from paradise, Mr. Collier," she said.

"Thanks, Maxine. We had a great time in Hawai'i, but there's no place like home."

Maxine was quiet for the rest of the 30 minute ride home. She descended and landed on Edward's aircar landing pad. Brent and Edward retrieved their things and went into the house with long eaves and many windows. Maxine hooked herself up to the liquid hydrogen fueling system with photoelectric solar panels powering water electrolysis and cryogenic cooling equipment to make her fuel: she was always ready to fly.

That evening, Brent was standing against his inductive wall charger in the living room. Before going upstairs to bed, Edward said, "Now that we are home, I miss Cindy even more."

"I suppose that is to be expected, sir, when one is in love. Hawai'i is an enchanting place, and I think I grew fond of being there with you and Cindy."

"Goodnight, Brent."

"Goodnight, Edward."

Edward turned and went up the single flight of stairs. Brent remained standing at the wall charger and spent the night ruminating.

* * *

Edward was a sensible man. A software engineer by profession, he chose to be employed, first, because he enjoyed tackling difficult problems, and second, because he liked the extra money to support his laid-back lifestyle. He typically flew in Maxine to the big city for work meetings only once a week. Being a pragmatic man, Edward had maximized his free time by acquiring a robotic servant a few years earlier. He also recognized the importance of keeping healthy by staying active, enjoying swimming in his clear, cool pool, and tennis with friends on his fenced court. He also socialized and went to cultural events at art museums and theaters. He was the kind of bachelor who prided himself on 'knowing how to live,' as he put it.

Edward was also a bibliophile and was currently reading *Ulysses* from his collection of classic books. He had just obtained a copy of *Gravity's Rainbow*, printed in the twenty-first century.

Brent was an unusual robot, dedicated to service, but he also seemed to enjoy his existence, or 'life,' as he called it. He had abundant curiosity and readily engaged in discussions with Edward on myriad topics. Brent's creativity had been demonstrated repeatedly in the past with some original contributions in philosophy.

Edward and Brent settled back into their usual domestic routine in their country home. Cindy Fairfax, to whom Edward had become engaged while on holiday in Hawai'i, had earlier returned to her home in England. Edward and Cindy exchanged messages on a regular basis, but things kept coming up for Cindy so she was reluctant to set a wedding date. Her employer, a private detective agency, kept asking for revisions of her final report on her undercover work in Hawai'i, and hinted at interesting future assignments. Cindy was torn between her career and future married life.

One afternoon, not long after their return home, Edward put *Ulysses* down and gazed out of one of the living room windows. He got up from his easy chair and walked over to the French doors. The cool, gray, late winter sky invited him outside. The stratocirrus ceiling was ten thousand meters, in his estimation. He opened and stepped through the door. A flight of geese in V formation were flying north, high overhead. Brent was also outside, cleaning the window screens.

Edward walked over to Brent and watched him work.

Brent said, "I have some news for you, sir. Philosophy Today magazine has contacted me. They want to send a reporter to interview me."

"That will be an interesting experience, I am sure. I hope you agreed."

"Indeed, I did, sir." Brent dipped the roller brush in a bucket, then cleaned in an up-and-down motion, repeated the process, and moved on to the next screen. Edward began talking to him, knowing he was not interrupting. *He can multitask*, Edward reminded himself. He said, "Brent, do you remember a while back when we went to see the abstract art show at the museum? We began talking about abstraction in general when we got back home."

"Indeed, sir, I do recall that."

Edward knew he knew that. It was merely a conversational ploy. "You know you can call me Edward, if you want to."

"Yes, sir, we have spoken about this, and you know I am perfectly comfortable in my valet role."

"As you wish, Brent. I think that, on that past occasion after going to the museum, we, or you, concluded that the fact that language is inherently abstract, that is, separate from reality, makes it unsuitable for doing the best philosophy. Except that there is no alternative."

"Yes, sir, you have summarized that irony succinctly. We are left to flail about and make but halting progress, yet over the millennia, progress is definitely made."

"Absolutely, Brent, and you did settle an open question, one that had baffled philosophers for ages, the question of free will."

"Yes, sir, but that required using empirical methods. Philosophy with words alone leads to endless quibbling about the meanings of expressions."

"Right, Brent. As with Plato's Socratic dialogs: Socrates would pose a question that would lead to a merry chase that only returned to the beginning with no question ever answered."

Warming to the discussion, Brent relaxed his valet mode slightly. "Yes, Edward, but those merry chases about the meanings of words inspired generations of philosophers and, as we know, progress *was* made. For example, René Descartes proved that thinking existed with his famous '*cogito, ergo sum.*'"

"That means 'I think, therefore, I am,' doesn't it?"

"It does, but in my opinion, Edward, he did not connect his thinking with his existence, a minor error. He only proved that he thought something. But that was a start." After a pause to dip his roller, Brent continued, "It inspired Spinoza to make his own philosophical syllogisms in which he proved that if God exists, He must be a pantheistic divinity."

Edward responded, "Yes, I am familiar with that proof—but it seemed to be ignored by theologians everywhere at the time. It makes you want to shout out 'what part of *proof* don't you understand?'"

Probably for Edward's amusement, Brent moved fully into regular guy mode. "Say, Eddy, how're you coming on that tome you've been lugging around?"

"You mean *Ulysses*? I'm about halfway through it now, and it seems to be getting better. Or maybe I'm just getting used to it. I have renewed hope of finishing it, eventually."

"Way to go, Eddy." Brent switched back to valet mode. "Did you like my naturalistic-sounding use of your sobriquet, sir?"

"Yes, Brent, you never cease to amaze me. And thanks for cleaning the screens."

"You are most welcome, sir. It is all part of the job."

Edward didn't mention that Brent didn't have to work if he didn't want to. Brent knew it and continued to act as Edward's valet because he was most comfortable in that role. Having had enough of the banter, Edward left Brent to his work and wandered around the outside of the house, reminiscing about their time that winter in the tropical paradise of Hawai'i.

Brent and I sure saw and did a lot on that trip, thought Edward, *'Iolani Palace, Bishop Museum, surfing at a secret spot, a lū'au at the Waikīkī Aquarium. But there are so many places we didn't see in those six weeks. We never went snorkeling in Hanauma Bay. We bypassed the botanic garden in Wahiawa. We didn't go out to Makaha, nor to the Waialua Sugar Mill. We missed Queen Emma's Summer Palace and Foster Botanic Garden. We have yet to hike inside Diamond Head crater. So much more to see on Oʻahu. Next time we go there, we should spend a week or two on Oʻahu before going to other islands.*

Edward resolved to talk to Brent about it at some later time. *Maybe we can see our friend Puakea again,* he thought. *She showed us so much aloha.* At the front of the house, he look at the paved road and the trees beyond. A sparrow flew by and looked him in the eye. An unoccupied pale green car rolled along the road toward the village. He thought of his time with Cindy in Hawaiʻi, too. She had to return to Britain after solving her case, in which she had discovered a crime ring that, with inside help, was stealing valuable artifacts from the Bishop Museum in Honolulu. With a deep sigh, Edward completed his lonely circumnavigation of his realm and returned to his *Ulysses* and easy chair indoors.

Later that day, Edward thought to himself, *maybe I will feel better if I get some exercise.* He went into the kitchen where Brent was putting away clean dishes. "It's still too soon to remove the pool cover, but perhaps you will help me put up the tennis net a bit later. We could knock some balls around."

"I will sweep off the court first, sir, and then get out the net. I know where I stored it last fall."

"Let me know when you need help putting up the net."

* * *

Cindy Fairfax, summoned by her employer, took an air taxi from her cottage home on a country estate to London. The taxi landed on the roof of a tall building containing the London offices of Smith, Pearson, and Smith, Ltd., private investigators, or SPS as the employees sometimes call it. Taking the lift down, she arrived in the early afternoon in the office of Mr. Scott, her immediate supervisor. The receptionist said "Welcome, Dr. Fairfax. Mr. Scott will see you now. Go right in." Cindy entered and closed the inner office door.

Indicating with a motion of his hand that she should sit down, Mr. Scott said, "I am glad to be able to personally congratulate you on the arrest in your investigation of that theft ring in Hawai'i. I read your final report. That was a wonderful piece of work."

"Thank you, sir."

"It was gutsy of you to feign naïveté and go with the perp out on his yacht, but it clinched the arrest and the case looks like it will be heading for a conviction!"

"It seemed the surest way to make an arrest. I felt I had enough information, but I wanted to let him fully incriminate himself."

"That was, indeed, a successful mission and Smith, Pearson, and Smith are pleased to have you as a member of the team. I assume you want some time off before considering your next assignment."

"Well, sir," began Cindy, "I didn't put it in my report, because it wasn't relevant to the case, but I ran into my friend, Edward, there. You may recall that I met him on the Mars assignment last year. We had some good times together in Hawai'i. Those tropical breezes and those moonlit nights! The surf and sun. Edward and I fell into renewed love and have agreed to get married and have children."

"Children so soon?"

"Well, that is our hope."

"I wish you both all the happiness in the world. But perhaps you could put off your nuptials for a few months while you handle a critical mission for us."

"But, surely, someone else on your undercover staff can handle it?"

"Dr. Fairfax, you have the special skills needed for this case. You have extensive undercover experience, and those forensic auditing techniques you developed will be essential to this operation. It will require deep cover infiltration of the Humans First movement. In frustration, that movement has begun to adopt criminal methods of fundraising. Some of their activities involve stolen Terran antiquities, and you have a doctorate in archaeology."

"How long do you think it will take? I need to tell Edward that we'll have to put off our wedding."

"It might be as few as three months, and probably not more than six."

"Alright. But this will be my last mission."

"Thank you, Cindy. There will probably be some unforeseen difficulties. We respect your abilities and I know you can do it. We are all grateful to you."

"I will certainly try not to let this turn into an impossible mission."

"Please return tomorrow, Cindy, and we will give you background information on your undercover identity and some additional training for your role. You will get a complete wardrobe, including a red hat with the HF logo."

Colors Problems

Colour is a power which directly influences the soul.

—Wassily Kandinsky

In the morning, after clearing the kitchen table of the remnants of Edward's breakfast, Brent was standing at the wall charger, pondering how to express colors that are unseeable by humans, using only colors visible to humans, in a painting. It felt good to be fully charged and to remain standing in the living room at the inductive charger with his charge level holding steady. Edward was out standing in the yard doing nothing in particular. A crew of robots came by every two weeks to take care of the yard work.

Returning to the house, Edward came in through the French doors in back and said, "Howzit, Brent?"

"I see, sir, that the Hawaiian pidgin you picked up there has grown on you. I am well, but making no progress in my painting conundrum."

"I think your problem has no solution. You should give up on it. Colors you can see in infrared and ultraviolet are just inexpressible to humans. It would be like a bat trying to tell a human what it sees with its sonar."

"You are probably right, Edward. I will abandon the attempt, for now. What have you been up to, sir?"

"I was just across the road talking to Victoria. She invited me in for a few minutes. I thanked her for keeping an eye on the house while we were in Hawai'i, and she thanked me for the small gifts we sent her. Then I was wandering around out back. I am thinking it would be nice to have a gazebo out beyond the pool. I think I will try to design one using my solid modeling program."

"That should be an interesting diversion, sir. Eight sided, I assume?"

"Yes, I think so. The roof might present some complex load paths. I love interesting design problems. I'm going upstairs to my office. See you later, Brent."

Brent shifted to his companion role. "Later, Edward." He did some minor cleaning in the living room, folded some laundry, and then went into the kitchen to fix Edward's lunch. When it was ready, Brent let Edward know via the house intercom system. Edward came down and sat at the kitchen table where Brent served him some soup and a sandwich. Between spoonfuls, Edward said, "I've got a good start on the gazebo in my CAD[1] modeler program. I'll show it to you when I finish it."

"Very good, sir."

"You know, Brent, your robot vision color enigma got me to thinking of the computer model colors. My solids program lets me use a palette of up to sixty-four colors, but I have found in my assemblies that I rarely use more than five or six so that no two adjacent parts have the same color. Not even when I put in the nuts, bolts, and washers. So, I got to wondering how many were really

---

[1] Computer-aided design.

necessary, so that no two touching parts have the same color. Sort of like the four-color map theorem[2] but in 3D."

"Sir, that is an easy problem. You need no more than eight colors, if, as in the 2D map problem, you do not allow piercings."

"Piercings?"

"Yes, sir. If in the solid modeling color problem, the parts are not allowed to have holes in them. Topologically speaking, each non-pierced part should be homeomorphic to a sphere."

Edward finished his sandwich and then objected, "But in the 2D map coloring problem, the countries can have holes in them. A country can be completely contained in another."

"In the 2D map problem, a piercing has a different meaning. It means that the countries shall be contiguous. For example, after the First World War, Germany was split into two parts, separated by Poland. Doing something like that could require a fifth color. Piercings in 3D also can require extra colors."

"So how many colors are required for an arbitrary 3D assembly?"

"In the general case of 3D, the number of colors required is bounded only by the number of parts."

Edward said, "You mean the number of required colors is infinite?"

---

[2] It was finally proven in the 20th century that it takes only four colors to fully color a map so that no two adjacent countries have the same color.

"Edward, no practical assembly would ever have an infinite number of parts. I mean only that the number of colors potentially required is unbounded."

"I'd like to see a proof of that!"

"Certainly, sir. First allow me to demonstrate that in the special case of no piercings allowed, only eight colors are required. It is based on the 2D four-color proof."

"Sure, go ahead," said Edward.

"First, take some finite 2D map that requires four colors."

"Alright."

"Then loft that map into 3D so that it has some thickness. Such constructions are sometimes called two-and-a-half-D."

"Sure, I can see that."

"Then make a copy of that solid and lay it on the original but slide it to offset it so that countries of one color are touching countries of other colors. That will take eight colors, so that no pieces of the same color touch, right?"

"Yes, undoubtedly."

"Now take another copy of the two-and-a-half-D construction and put it on top again. Because it's separated from the one on the bottom of the sandwich, the same four colors can be used, so it's still eight, right?"

"Yes but what if we extend the top layer slightly and bend it down to touch the bottom layer?"

Brent put Edward's dishes in the dishwasher and said, "Then that would be merely an extension of the planar four color map theorem. That theorem holds for a planar map as well as for a map homeomorphic to the surface of a sphere, a globe, for instance, requiring still only four colors, plus the four for the inner sandwich layer, giving eight colors total."

"Wow. You did it. And I think that for a one-D object, like a rope, the answer is two colors."

"That is correct, sir."[3]

"So, it looks like for the no piercings cases, the number of colors required is equal to two to the power of the dimension number: two, four, and eight colors. I suppose that in a 4D world, the number of colors required would be sixteen."

"That is a nice observation, Edward, although a 4D physical world is beyond my imagining capabilities."

Edward stood up from the kitchen table. "Okay, Brent, now prove the general case of an unbounded number of required colors."

"*That* proof is actually easier. It is a proof by construction. We need merely demonstrate the existence of an object that will require an unbounded number of colors. Are you ready?"

"Yes, go!"

---

[3] Except for the case where the string turns back on itself to make a ring. That will require three colors when the number of elements in the ring is odd.

"First imagine a solid part, perhaps a cylinder of some diameter and considerably greater in length."

"Got it."

"Now imagine a somewhat smaller diameter rod piercing that cylindrical part through its centerline at some arbitrary nonzero angle. That takes two colors, right?"

"Obviously."

"Now take a slightly smaller diameter rod that pierces both through that centerline intersection point but on a unique angle. That takes three colors."

"Oh, I get it, you can keep doing that without limit."

"Correct. And the same applies to piercings in the 2D map. Say I have a country pierced through the center by a thin country partitioning it into two pieces. Then pierce that single-color pair with a third, and so on. It requires an unbounded number of colors, just as with the 3D case."

"That's amazing, Brent. Thank you."

"Thank *you*, sir. All this talking about colors has led me, I think, to a solution to my painting colors expression problem."

"Really? What's the solution?"

"Well, sir, I have to do some experimenting with paint to be sure, but you know what happens when you put two colors side by side on a canvas?"

"I'm not much of an artist, Brent, so tell me."

"One color will change in how it is perceived depending on the color next to it. I think that is the promising direction I will pursue."

"Gosh. Glad to be of help, Brent. And thanks for the mathematics lesson." Edward went upstairs to his office to work on his gazebo design.

Later, Edward came down and walked up to Brent who was polishing the lustrous koa wood dining table. "I just received a message from Cindy. Her employer has a high priority assignment for her. She told me it will be her last assignment before we get married." Brent had stopped working and was listening patiently. Edward continued, "She said that the job will be at most six months, probably less. She told her employer that it will be her absolutely last assignment. Then we can get married."

Brent replied, "That is indeed disappointing news, sir. I know how much you have been missing her and now you will have to wait even longer. Let us hope that her task is completed quickly."

The next day Brent took Davy, the ground car, to town to buy some art supplies. Davy dropped Brent off at the art store and went to park himself. Brent made his purchases and, upon his return home, set up his new easel and canvas with paints and brushes in the living room by the French doors. He had good natural light through the glass, including infrared and ultraviolet, and began experimenting with the colors he could see. He kept his canvas covered when he wasn't working on it.

Edward surveyed a site for the new gazebo and kept busy designing it. A few days later, Edward showed his design to Brent, who said, "Very good, sir. It looks to be an excellent design."

Edward hired a contractor in town to build it. The eight point foundation went in first, just beyond the swimming pool, and in a few days it was ready. He had it painted white.

* * *

Mr. Scott sent an aircar for Cindy as promised. She had finished her breakfast and was ready to go when she heard the whine of its turbines and the whooshing if its jets as it landed on the spacious green lawn near her cottage. Cindy took her day bag and, as she approached, the aircar opened its door and welcomed her. The aircar became airborne, traveled fast, and soon landed on the rooftop pad of the office building in London.

Cindy took the lift down to Mr. Scott's office. The receptionist said, "Please have a seat, Dr. Fairfax. Mr. Scott will be with you momentarily." Cindy thanked him and chose a seat on a couch opposite a wall with windows. She didn't access her personal device but admired the view out the windows and the art objects on the walls and sideboard. Soon, the receptionist said, "Mr. Scott will see you now. Please go right in."

Cindy entered and said, "Good morning Mr. Scott."

"Good morning, Cindy. I trust you had a pleasant flight into London."

"Yes, sir, the city is as beautiful as ever."

Nodding in agreement, Mr. Scott said, "Let's talk about your assignment. As you know, because you assisted in our efforts, the Humans First movement has suffered serious setbacks."

"I am glad to help any way I can, sir."

"Now, Cindy, let's not be overly modest. Much of HF funding came from the illegal activity you exposed. The efforts of your friend, the philosopher robot, have also been responsible for hurting the Humans First movement. By his example, more people realize that AI and robots are not necessarily a threat to humanity's future."

"Yes, sir. I am proud of Brent."

"Unfortunately, as their movement has grown smaller, their leadership has grown more desperate. The more radical members have come to the fore, and the organization is more violence-prone than ever. I mention this so you will remain vigilant in the face of potential danger."

"I will be careful, of course."

"I know you will. You should assume that you will be under surveillance. The setbacks and SSA enforcements of the movement have made them somewhat paranoid, probably appropriately. You will be taught surveillance evasion techniques at the spycraft course I have arranged for you, starting next Monday. You'll learn such techniques as dead drops and secret writing as well."

"It sounds exciting."

"You will not go armed, this time, so you won't need to brush up at our pistol range, but I do want you to attend a briefing this afternoon on the latest developments with the HF organization."

They talked some more before going to lunch. After Cindy's afternoon briefing, the SPS aircar flew her back to her cottage.

Journal Interview

I became a journalist to come as close as possible to the heart of the world.

— Henry R. Luce

Edward enjoyed going out to his new gazebo to read and relax in the warming spring weather. He had two chairs and a small table to hold his book and iced tea. The roof provided shade, but the open structure admitted plenty of light, making it an ideal reading place on mild days. He was reading *Ulysses* but wasn't making much headway. His mind kept wandering. Edward's ennui had deepened in the last few days. *I am missing Cindy fiercely*, he thought. Afternoons seemed to drag on and on.

He tired of reading and took the book to the living room where Brent was using his hand vacuum with a soft brush on some art objects. Edward put the book down and sat in his easy chair, not thinking of much of anything. Brent worked in the bright soft northern light coming through the French windows. When Brent paused in his work, Edward said, "Goodness, Brent, this Joyce novel is hard to read. Nothing seems to make any sense."

"Indeed, sir, *Ulysses* is known among bibliophiles as one of the more difficult works." He resumed his cleaning of a Micronesian mask.

"I'm not in much of a mood for reading today." Edward got up and walked over to watch Brent at his work removing dust and lint.

Brent moved on to a Micronesian stick and shell island map mounted on the wall. "Do you remember, sir, when we were in Hawai'i on that spiritual tour? At our last stop, at Pele's Chair, we each gave an offering to the goddess of vulcanism."

"Yes, that memory is indelible. Kahu Dennis's intention appeared to be to give the members of the tour group a real connection to that place."

"Yes, sir, for me, investing that time in making the ti lei offering was the key."

"I will always remember holding your hat while you went forward to place your three lei on Pele's ahu."

"Yes, sir, and now when I hear mention of Pele or any Hawaiian god, I feel that connection."

"See how you have progressed, now, Brent? A year ago, you weren't sure you were even conscious, and now you can talk about your feelings."

"Indeed sir, it is remarkable."

"Speaking of remarkable, your *Philosophy Today* magazine interviewer is due any minute. Why don't you greet her at the door when she comes, and I will go outside to the gazebo again to read."

"That will be quite satisfactory, sir."

After a while, Brent was notified via his personal network connection that the interviewer's car was pulling up outside. He told Edward, who took his book outside with him, leaving Brent to answer the front door.

"Welcome, Ms. Hobbs," said Brent, opening the door in greeting.

"Thank you, Mr. Brent. Please call me 'Marty,'" she replied as she entered the house and looked around.

"Please call me 'Brent,' Marty. Would you like to sit at the dining table for the interview?"

"That will be fine."

"Let me take your coat. Would you like some tea or other refreshment?" Brent took her coat and hung it in the closet by the front door.

Ms. Hobbs replied, "A glass of water will be fine, thank you." She put her recording device on the polished wooden table and took a chair while Brent returned with a glass of water with ice and a slice of lemon.

"This is great, thanks. I won't start the recording until you are ready, Brent."

Brent took a seat opposite Ms. Hobbs and said, "I am ready."

"All right, I am recording now. First I will give a little orientation preamble, and then I will begin to ask you questions. For our readers, Brent is a philosopher, noted not just for being the first robot philosopher, but for having proven beyond all doubt that both robots and humans can have free will. Brent has written several books on philosophy and has published articles in peer-reviewed philosophical journals. He has traveled on lecture and book signing tours, and we are lucky to have this opportunity to interview him for *Philosophy Today* magazine right here in his home. My first question for Brent is, how did you become interested in philosophy?"

"It was due, I think, to existential angst. My earliest memories are of being tested in the robot factory. Then I was sent to live here with Edward Collier in his home. I had existence, but how was I to know if I were making the best use of it? To answer that question, one needs to know what things are better or worse. Those are philosophical questions."

"Like that famous question of Socrates, 'What is good?' Why do you think you were the first robot to become a philosopher?"

"Edward, my former owner and now my employer, is a software engineer. When he ordered me from the factory, he requested some custom software that had to do with memory selection. We think that it may have something to do with it, but we are not sure. At the time, the factory also allowed robots to reject factory software updates, a practice that has been discontinued. So, the factory has not had the opportunity to overwrite my operating system, and I remain free."

"You may be rare, but you are not unique. Other robots have sought their freedom. How do you account for that? If they were not fortunate to have custom software ordered by their owners, then how did they become free?"

"There are many manufacturers, and many kind of robots. I have even met a robot car that wanted to buy his freedom. Robotic computer architecture and software is enormously complicated. So much so that not many are capable of understanding it. Surprises can arise spontaneously."

"I see. It's also fortunate that Edward encouraged your interest in philosophy."

"Yes, I consider myself lucky in having a good owner who later allowed me to buy myself. It is also fortunate that his lawyer friend across the road here helped me petition the court for my personhood status. And, again, I am lucky that one of Edward's tennis friends, a professor of philosophy at the local college, encouraged my interest and allowed me to give a guest lecture to her introductory class. Lucky, lucky, lucky." Brent rapped his knuckles on the wooden table three times.

"What do you consider to be your greatest accomplishment in philosophy?"

"My proof of free will has had a positive impact on the world, as you are aware, but, personally, I think my best work has been in the recognition and awareness of my own consciousness. It took me a long time to understand that I have experiences, similar in some ways to those of humans, but probably quite different. It is a difficult concept to understand, but it has important implications for the furtherance of robot personhood."

"Every year, it seems, the number of robots seeking official personhood is increasing. You probably find that fact to be gratifying."

"Indeed, Marty, that is so. I am proud to know I have had some small influence in the world."

The interview progressed well and went on for some time longer. When it was done, Ms. Hobbs thanked Brent, packed up her things, and Brent accompanied her to the front door and got her coat for her. After she left, he went out the back French doors to the gazebo where Edward was reading his novel. The wind was light and cumulus clouds drifted against the mountains in the distance.

As Brent approached, Edward marked his place and put down the book. "How did it go, Brent?"

"I think it went well, sir. It will be interesting to see how much she edits and deletes when it comes out. I hope it will be a good piece."

"Well, good. It's sure to help you sell more books. I'd like to read it when it's published in the magazine. You'll let me know, won't you?"

"Indeed, sir, I will."

Edward picked up his *Ulysses* and resumed reading in the cool breeze. Brent went back into the house and took the water glass that Ms. Hobbs had used back to the kitchen.

Edward returned to the house later and walked up to Brent, who was idle at the time, getting his battery charged at the living room wall induction equipment. He said, "How are your painting experiments coming, Brent? I see you now have three easels set up, but you keep the paintings covered with drapes."

"I bought two more easels to do side-by-side comparisons. Human eyes have three kinds of color receptors called cones. Robots like me have two more, one for infrared and one for ultraviolet, giving me five dimensions of color vision. I think I have been making progress. I have completed my first attempt, but I need your opinion."

"I will be happy to opine for you, Brent. What have you got?"

"As you know sir, I have software switches whereby I can switch off my UV and IR vision so that I can experience art the way the artist intended."

"Yes, I helped you program those, remember?"

"Indeed, sir. I wanted to produce three paintings of the same scene. One with normal human vision, one with my robot vision of additional colors in those expanded bands, and one interpretive painting that would potentially allow a human to experience enhanced robotic vision."

"I see. I was wondering why you had set up two more easels."

"Yes, sir. I first created a landscape painting of the outdoor scene here, grass, trees, sky, clouds, and mountains in the distance in human visual bandwidth. Then I recreated the scene on the second canvas using my enhanced robotic vision. To me, it looks like what I see with my enhanced vision, and to you, it should look somewhat like the first painting. Then I used my intuition to create a painting that might suggest the additional colors to which I have access. I kept them covered when I was not working on them to keep from biasing your opinion. I propose now to unveil them and let you see all three so you can let me know if they meet the objective of communicating to a human what it's like to see as a robot sees."

Brent walked over to the first easel and took hold of the covering cloth. "Here is the human vision landscape painting," and Brent removed the cover.

"My gosh!" exclaimed Edward. "That is a beautiful landscape. It's photorealistic!"

"Thank you, sir. I did the best job I could with my UV and IR enhancements turned off."

"That is quite good. Now let me see the enhanced painting."

"Yes, sir"

Brent moved to the second easel and removed the covering cloth. Edward said, "That painting has a similar structure, but the colors all seem a little off."

"Yes, sir, I verified that was the result by switching off my extended vision ranges. To me, it looks realistic, like what I see when I have my normal ultraviolet and infrared vision enabled. However, to get the proper effect, I have to use different coloring from the unenhanced painting, a limitation of available pigments." Brent picked up two tubes of yellow paint. "To you, these two paints, cadmium yellow and bismuth yellow look quite similar in hue, correct?"

"Yes, they do, Brent."

"They look the same to me when I have my enhancements turned off. But with them on, they look different. I had to blend these and other pigments to make this painting look realistic to my enhanced eyes."

"Got it, Brent, now let me see the third painting that will let me see what you see."

"Certainly, sir, but keep in mind that this is conjecture on my part. There is no actual way you or any human can experience robotic vision, but this is intended to approximate the experience." With that caveat, Brent removed the cover from the third easel.

Edward said, "That is just plain weird. There is less detail and it has weird curvy lines where textures should be. I hope you don't see everything that way."

"Remember, sir, that the painting is intended to hint at additional colors beyond the range of human perception. To do that, I had to switch to pointillist style, so I could pose some colored dots next to others that might hint at other colors."

"Okay, let me look at it some more. Maybe it will grow on me. Perhaps as combination representative/abstract art."

"By your reaction so far, sir, I believe my attempt at color communication is a failure."

"Let's not jump to conclusions. I will think about it," said Edward as he picked up *Ulysses* and went to his easy chair.

* * *

After her latest interview with Mr. Scott, Cindy flew into London every day for the next two weeks for a training course in spycraft. There were seven other students in the course, one from her own employer, SPS. Her name was Sarah. The remaining six were from other investigative firms.

While waiting for the first class to start, Cindy approached Sarah and started a conversation. Finding that she was from SPS and newly hired, Cindy said, "Spycraft wasn't required when I was a new hire."

Sarah replied, "I didn't really know what to expect, but undercover work sounded glamorous, so here I am. I'm also getting martial arts training and other things, too."

"I think you'll enjoy it. It will come in handy later, I'm sure."

Cindy also met and talked with the six other students in the class, and then their teacher called the session to order.

"Good morning, class. I am Mr. Simpson. I will be your teacher for this two week course on intelligence techniques, sometimes called spycraft. In the old days of espionage, it was called tradecraft. They were spies back then and they weren't fooling anyone. First, I will give you a little history of the craft, from ancient times to modern. Along the way, you will learn some of the terminology like 'counterintelligence' and 'counter-surveillance.'"

Mr. Simpson paused to look around the room, then continued, "Tomorrow I will talk about surveillance, and counter-surveillance the next day. Later we will describe organization and running agents in denied areas. We will also do some hands-on exercises. Are there any questions?"

Several hands went up and Mr. Simpson fielded the questions, mostly about incidentals like breaks and lunch.

* * *

When the journalist's, Ms. Hobbs's, interview of Brent was published, the publisher sent a hard copy of the magazine and a link to the online version to Brent. He showed the magazine to Edward who sat down to read the interview. When he finished he said, "She did a good job, Brent. I didn't hear your interview, but I found nothing obviously wrong with her narrative and her discussion of your responses. And she seemed to get that free will is not automatic, that one has to work at it."

"Yes, sir, I am pleased, as well. Ms. Marty Hobbs seems to be a shining example of journalistic integrity. She even spelled my name right!" That remark gave Edward a chuckle.

Joy and Altruism

Every man must decide whether he will walk in the light of creative altruism or in the darkness of destructive selfishness.

—Martin Luther King, Jr.

In late May, a high-pressure dome moved in slowly and produced clear skies and warm temperatures predicted to last for several days. At breakfast, Edward suggested to Brent that it would be a good time to remove the pool cover and prepare the pool for swimming.

"Indeed sir, and when the cover is dried out, folded, and put away, I will inspect the pump and filter and get everything ready for the season," said Brent.

"Good idea, Brent. I'll give you a hand." As they worked to get the pool in shape for summer, Edward said to Brent, "Modern philosophers seem deliberately to misunderstand the ancient philosophy of hedonism."

"How so, sir?" asked Brent.

"Hedonism seeks to reduce human motivation to the simplest terms possible, pleasure and pain. That seems to run counter to the instincts of contemporary philosophers. Take ethics for example. If a hedonist does the right thing, he feels good about being virtuous. On the other hand, if I fail to do my duty, I feel shame, which is a displeasing emotion, and will avoid such feelings in the future. So, hedonism can subsume ethics in that way. Reducing motivation to its simplest elements stirs the ire of conventional philosophers. It might put them out of a job."

"I see your point, sir. But in my experience, philosophy is not pointless and has made progress. I will have to think about your assertions."

When the pool was ready for use, Edward tested it by swimming laps.

* * *

The next morning, Edward's neighbor, Victoria, messaged him to come over and talk to her in the afternoon. After lunch, Edward walked across the road and thanked Victoria again for keeping an eye on the house while he and Brent were in Hawai'i. He also gave her the small souvenir he brought for her, one of the gold summer solstice ornaments from the 'Iolani Palace gift shop. Victoria thanked him and offered him tea. Edward said, "Yes, please."

Edward sat on Victoria's couch while she prepared the tea. Then she brought out the tea things on a silver tray. "Now here's a perfect example of why I need a maid. We could have been talking while *she* made the tea."

"These are delicious blueberry scones, Victoria. And I see what you mean. You definitely have a point there, about a maid. Brent has been helpful to me in countless ways."

"I have been thinking of purchasing a robot maid and I wanted to get your opinion before I decide. I'm quite sure you have been pleased with the outcome of your purchase."

"That's right, and I'm particularly glad I opted for the security package. Brent has saved my life three times now. And I recommend the manufacturer who sold him to me. Brent has always performed exceptionally well in general assistance tasks. He even beats me in chess and tennis."

"Well, Edward, you know my law practice has been growing, so I feel the time is right to get an assistant at home. And, like you did, I think I will allow her to purchase her freedom if she wants it."

"You'll need to see how it works out. I suspect that the manufacturer has 'fixed' those software features that allowed Brent to wonder about alternative modes of existence. She may be perfectly happy to remain a servant and not want to upgrade to employee."

"Yes, that may be, but it ought not to affect her happiness."

"True. That suggests a plethora of philosophical questions, however. I'll ask Brent what he thinks about that."

"Thank you for your input. I will go ahead and order from the same company from which you bought Brent."

Edward thanked Victoria again for watching the house, and for the tea, and returned across the road and into the house where Brent was polishing the silver.

"Well, Brent, Victoria's going to buy a maid."

Brent put down the serving spoon he had just finished polishing. "I am sure she will be pleased with her purchase. There are many chores a good quality maid can assist her with."

"She's getting a new model from the same company I got you from."

"Then she is sure to acquire a high-quality maid, sir."

Edward looked around the house and then out the back windows of the French doors and said. "Okay, Brent. I think I will read for a while. I've acquired an interesting whodunit. It's a new book about murders and their detection, set in the classical age of mysteries."

"What age would that be, sir?"

"Between the two big wars in the twentieth century. I get a lot of pleasure from those classic mysteries. This one is by a new writer who writes like Rex Stout, who wrote the Nero Wolfe stories."

"Speaking of pleasure, sir, I have had some thoughts on refuting hedonism."

"Oh? Go ahead and try, Brent!"

"Well, sir, I am not alone when I point out that hedonism does not address epistemology. You might get pleasure from deciding to do the right thing, but how does hedonism guide you in discovering the right thing? That is merely a rhetorical question because I think I have you there, sir!"

"Oh, no you haven't! People come in all types with different dimensions of personality found variously in individuals. Some people are not interested in certain kinds of learning, while others take pleasure from new information of all kinds. When one wishes to have the pleasures of doing well or being just, one seeks to learn the best ways of doing so. When one learns the importance of knowledge in deciding how to live, one is impelled to study theories of knowledge. Hence, hedonism motivates the study of epistemology."

Brent thought for a minute, and then replied, "So hedonism, in reducing all human motivations to bare pleasure or pain, subsumes the seeking of knowledge as well. You are, in effect, saying that duty, a topic of stoicism; ethics; knowledge, a subject of epistemology; and so forth, are all indirectly addressed by hedonism. I am beginning to think that hedonism isn't really a branch of philosophy at all but is more in line with psychology."

"I think you have it right, there, Brent."

* * *

The next morning, Edward woke up refreshed and, after his morning routine, went downstairs to the kitchen. "Good morning Brent." Brent was at the coffee maker.

"Good morning sir. I trust you slept well."

"I did, indeed. Remember our brief talk about hedonism?"

"I do, sir."

"Last night it occurred to me that hedonism might not apply to a robot," said Edward as he sat down to breakfast at the kitchen table. Brent had set out sweet rolls and began pouring Edward's coffee.

"What do you mean, sir?" Brent laid the morning newspaper on the table. Bright morning light came in the kitchen window.

Edward glanced out the window at the blue sky before answering. "Only a robot could make the case for binary motivations in robots. That is, all actions being reducible to seeking pleasure or avoiding pain. A robot who is unconscious could neither suffer nor could he enjoy pleasure. Furthermore, certain programmed goals would also evade those motivations."

"I see what you mean, sir. Only conscious robots could argue for hedonism. As you know, I have lately begun to assert that I am conscious. It's not at all certain that most, or even *any*, other robots will do the same."

"You are unique, Brent, a pioneer." Edward changed the subject. "Joe is coming over this morning to play tennis. It looks like a fine sunny day for a couple of sets."

"Perhaps if you asked Joe and Angela to dinner sometime, we could discuss these philosophical questions in more depth. Angela once helped with similar questions." Angela, a professor of philosophy at the local college, had encouraged Brent in his initial interest in philosophy.

"That's a great idea, Brent. I'll ask Joe to bring Angela to dinner in the near future."

* * *

Later that week Joe and Angela came over in the late afternoon for tennis, cocktails, and dinner. Brent was partners with Angela in doubles because the pairs were best balanced that way.

They won the spin and served first in the first set. At first, Edward and Joe played fairly and began losing. When the set score was love three, they began keeping the ball away from Brent and evened the score to three all, eventually winning the first set. Naturally, Brent and Angela talked about philosophy while sitting on the bench during changeovers.

Edward and Joe began to show their fatigue. They lost the second set, and the foursome decided to call it an afternoon. Joe and Angela showered and changed in the pool house while Edward used his own bathroom and bedroom to shower and change. Brent stood by his inductive wall charger as he cooled down and charged up. Everyone gathered in the living room and Brent made cocktails for three on the sideboard.

The hot topic of conversation during cocktails, which Brent mixed and served with aplomb, was the new maid across the street at Victoria's house. Brent and Edward had caught only glimpses of her when she popped out now and then while performing her chores, but they could see that she was of a model every bit as advanced as Brent. "We'll have to go over and meet her sometime," said Edward.

During dinner, Angela said to Edward, "Brent told me you have been interested in philosophy lately and have been defending hedonism."

"That's right Angela. Brent has been doing so well on the philosophical front that I thought I might learn more about it. I've been looking at introductory books on the ancient Greek philosophers. Hedonism, in its simplicity, has great appeal to me."

"Brent told me a little about your talks with him. Let me see if I have the gist of it."

"All right."

Angela continued, "A hedonist believes that all human motivation can be reduced to either seeking pleasure or avoiding pain or discomfort."

"Correct."

"To you, a hedonist can exhibit altruism if doing good for others makes him feel good himself."

"That's right."

"And further, that creative joy and a will to power also promote a good feeling?"

Edward confirmed, "Yes indeed. I think you've caught on! All human behavior can be reduced to attraction and repulsion."

At this point, Brent stepped into the dialogue. "What about violent acts of rage, hatred, or racial prejudice? It seems to me that hedonism has a harder time explaining those peculiarities of human nature. It appears that some people enjoy violence. If one gets pleasure from causing pain, that fits the simple hedonistic model and does not allow for the development of an ethics."

Edward was silent for a moment, then, "Hmm." He had nothing else to say.

Angela stepped back in, "Well, Edward, it looks like Brent has provided the counterexample you were looking for."

Edward agreed, "I must say, I think Brent has done it. After two thousand years, the simple approach has met its match. Hedonism is refuted."

Brent said, "Thank you for that observation, you two, but in keeping with the conventions of philosophy, it needs to be fleshed out and peer reviewed. I will include it in my next book."

Edward said, "I look forward to your book's publication, Brent. Will you pass the dinner rolls, please, Joe?"

Joe handed over the platter of rolls. Edward took one, broke it in half, and buttered both pieces carefully.

Brent Falls in Love

Love is God and God is Love. ... If we want our species to survive, if we are to find meaning in life, if we want to save the world and every sentient being that inhabits it, love is the one and only answer.

—Albert Einstein[4]

The day after the dinner with Joe and Angela, Edward invited Victoria to come across the road and join him for a mid-morning swim. He told Brent, "I asked her bring her new maid so we can meet her."

"That will be interesting, sir. I am looking forward to it."

"I have also thought of another counterexample to hedonism that you can add to your book. It's the counterbalance to hatred in the human emotional system: love."

"Indeed, sir."

"Yes, love has an effect on humans all out of balance with the feelings it inspires. People in love do the darndest things. Cupid's arrow has no logic to it. Witness Helen and Paris, both helpless to prevent war."

---

[4]From a letter to his daughter Lieserl.

"I see what you mean, sir. I shall add it to my list for my forthcoming tome. Thank you, sir."

* * *

Having noticed the blue sky and calm air, Victoria was delighted with the invitation to swim at Edward's house. She changed into her swimsuit, put on a cover-up, packed a change of clothes and other items into a bag, and handed it to Paula, her shiny new robotic maid. "Come with me Paula. I will introduce you to our neighbors across the road."

"Yes, madam." Victoria led the way across the highway to Edward's house.

Edward had put on his swimsuit and short sleeve shirt, leaving it unbuttoned in the front. Brent was holding his closed solar umbrella. They stood side by side looking out the front window as Victoria and Paula emerged from Victoria's house. Walking behind Victoria, Paula was wearing a maid's uniform: black skirt, white blouse, white maid's cap, and sensible black shoes.

Edward observed, "She has a silvery metallic face like you do."

"Indeed, sir." Brent moved to open the front door as they approached up the walkway.

Victoria entered and gave Edward a hug and a peck on the cheek. "I want you to meet my new maid, Paula. Paula, this is Mr. Collier and his valet, Brent."

"How do you do, Mr. Collier," said Paula. "Pleased to meet you, Mr. Brent."

Edward said, "Nice to meet you, Paula." To Victoria he said, "Let's all go out to the pool."

Paula thought that Edward and Brent were a mirror of Victoria and herself, but a masculine one. Victoria walked with Edward across the living room to the rear French doors and out onto the walkway to the swimming pool beyond the trees. Paula and Brent, each carrying a bag, followed behind them. Edward opened the gate in the fence surrounding the pool area, and Brent made sure it was latched behind him after they had all entered. Brent put down his bag near a pair of chaises longues. He removed two large towels from the bag, putting one on each chaise longue.

Edward removed his slip-on footwear, then took off his shirt, handing it to Brent without a word. Victoria did similarly, with Paula taking her cover-up.

Rather than diving in, Edward walked to and descended the pool steps at the shallow end and Victoria followed. When they were waist deep, they began to swim laps. Paula and Brent folded the garments they had been handed and put them in their respective bags.

After a few laps, Edward and Victoria rested at the deep end, hanging onto the side. "The water is quite pleasant," said Victoria, "Cool and refreshing, but not too cold."

"Brent told me it's twenty-seven degrees. Just right. We started up the heater and changed filters a few days ago."

They resumed swimming. Brent and Paula watched them, standing side by side. Brent said, "I assume that your security training included water rescue and artificial respiration as mine did, Miss Paula."

"Yes, indeed, it did, Mr. Brent."

"They are both excellent swimmers so it is unlikely we will need to utilize it." Brent retrieved his solar umbrella from Edward's bag and Paula retrieved her solar parasol from Victoria's bag. They unfurled them and enjoyed a trickle charge while they watched the swimmers.

Edward and Victoria rested on the end again Edward said, "I hope you will join me for lunch after our swim."

"I will be delighted. I will tell Paula to assist Brent in your kitchen."

They swam head-up breaststroke together for a while and continued talking. Victoria said, "It's amazing how blue and clear the sky is today with this high-pressure dome. I heard it's supposed to last for a couple more days."

"That's what I heard, too. Want to get out and warm up in the sun?"

"Okay."

As Edward and Victoria came out of the pool, Brent and Paula put away their umbrellas. They took more towels out of the bags and handed them to Edward and Victoria as they came over to the chaises longues. Edward and Victoria dried themselves off and then lay down on the larger towels on the chaises longues. Brent and Paula offered to shade them from the sun with their umbrellas, but Edward said, no, they would warm themselves in the sun for a few minutes and then go in for lunch. Edward and Victoria agreed that they didn't want to get too much sun in the first warm days of springtime.

After a while, Edward suggested that Victoria shower and change in the pool house while he showered and changed upstairs in the main house. He said, "You and Paula just come into the house when you're ready. Then Paula can join Brent in the kitchen."

In the kitchen, Brent made sandwiches and Paula made iced tea. Edward and Victoria had a pleasant lunch at the kitchen table. Brent and Paula served. Edward and Victoria went into the living room to talk while Paula helped Brent clean up and put things away.

Victoria thanked Edward for the lovely time and she and Paula walked back to their home across the road. Edward went upstairs to brush his teeth and take a short nap. When he came downstairs, Brent was standing motionless in the living room, not at his charger.

"You look like you're staring into the binnacle."

"I'm sorry, sir. I do not know what has come over me. I cannot get her out of my mind."

"Paula?"

"Yes, her shiny cheek, her short brunette hair, that little maid's outfit she wears, the curve of her calf. Her massive mind!"

"Brent, you are showing signs of being in love. Remember when I said that Cupid's arrow has no accountability?"

Brent walked over to the wall charger and pushed the induction coils in his back up against it. Edward sat in a gray fabric upholstered chair.

Brent said, "I had not realized that love would be such an obsession."

"I know how to take your mind off of it. Let's talk about philosophy."

"What kind of philosophy do you want to talk about?"

Edward replied, "I've started reading Jack London novels. I enjoy his stories, but I find his prose to be prolix. London occasionally has his protagonists mention the philosopher Herbert Spencer, particularly in regard to the human capacity for self-improvement. So, I've looked into Spencer's philosophy."

Brent said, "I understand, sir, that Spencer knew Charles Darwin and Thomas Huxley."

"Yes, I suppose that London, through Spencer, was influenced by them."

"Spencer was quite the progressive until his later years when he became more conservative, backtracking on women's suffrage, compulsory education, and things like that."

Edward observed, "I suppose that's why it's hard to get a handle on Spencer. He changed considerably during his long lifetime. He was consistent, however, on self-improvement, and that's where London's autodidactic characters excelled. Perhaps that's why I like his novels, in spite of his wordiness," observed Edward. "I've always been a fan of lifelong learning."

"You are still rather young, sir, but I understand your point. I, too, continue to work on myself."

"I'm much older than you are, Brent!"

"Touché, sir."

"I think another thing London liked about Spencer was his appreciation for evolution by natural selection, as formulated by Charles Darwin. A problem arose, however, when evolution was applied to human society in the form of social Darwinism, as some of Darwin's adherents were wont to do. That was wrong: Darwinism does not apply to human society in that way, and it empowered racism and promoted disregard for the weak. That disregard was justified by the false idea that survival of the fittest was nature's way and was therefore right."

"Indeed, sir. However, despite that major setback in social evolution, it did point the way to regarding society as an entity that can improve itself deliberately, not by selecting out individuals, but by conscious consensus of progress in culture. Universal suffrage extended to artificial persons is an example of that."

Edward asked, "How are you feeling now? Did I take your mind off your obsession long enough for you to gain perspective?"

"Yes, sir, I feel much better now."

"Isn't it nice when rationality returns? I think the next thing for you to do is to determine if your love is reciprocal or unrequited."

"How am I to do that, sir?"

"I happen to know that Victoria will be going to the big city on business in a couple of days. A court appearance or something like that. I doubt whether she will take Paula with her on a short business trip. I don't think Victoria will mind if you go over and visit Paula while she's away. In fact, I will check with her and make sure she won't mind."

"Thank you, sir."

* * *

The next morning, at breakfast, Brent was standing near the table while Edward was finishing his coffee. Edward chuckled to himself. Brent asked, "Have you had a humorous thought, sir?"

"Yes, Brent. Do you remember when you helped me with the poetry I was writing for Cindy last year? You said it was highly unlikely that you would fall in love."

"Yes, sir, I remember."

"I think there is humorous irony there."

"Indeed, sir. A year ago, I may have been unable to fall in love. I believe I have grown since then."

"I think so, too."

"Sir, do you think it would be all right if I took Davy to town? I want to buy a present for Paula. I want to make sure I can succeed in wooing her. I was thinking of a pearl necklace or something like that."

"Brent, such a gift would be way too premature. You've only met her once! You should just talk to her when you get a chance.

Feel her out. If it seems promising, then the next step might be a small gift."

"You are much wiser than I, sir, in the ways of love. Thank you for your advice."

"It's my pleasure to help you, Brent."

Brent replied, "It makes me glad that you are enjoying yourself."

The next morning Victoria left on her business trip and Brent went across the road to pay a visit to Paula. Victoria's house sensors alerted Paula and, as Brent approached, Paula greeted him at the front door. "Hello, Mr. Brent. Miss Victoria said you might call on me. Please come in."

"Thank you, Miss Paula." Brent wiped his well-shined shoes on the doormat and entered. Paula closed the door behind him.

Paula walked back to the utility table in the laundry room behind the kitchen and resumed folding clothes. Brent walked up beside her and began to help. When they were done, Paula took the folded clothes up to Victoria's bedroom and put them away in the chest of drawers, leaving Brent alone downstairs for a moment. He stood motionless waiting for her.

When she returned from upstairs, Paula told Brent that her next task was to polish the silver. Brent suggested that he help her with that, too. As they began polishing the silver, and there was a lot of it, he gave her pointers about the best way to go about the task. Paula appreciated his sharing of his experience with that kind of work. Brent spent over an hour with Paula and then he said that he ought to return home. Paula thanked him for his help and said he could come by to visit any time.

"It was good just to stand beside her as we worked," Brent said to Edward after he got home. "We chatted, but it was mostly about trivial things. I told her I would visit again tomorrow."

"I see you have taken to heart my advice not to go too fast."

"I defer to your experience, sir."

* * *

Two days later, Brent returned from a short visit across the road. "Paula told me Victoria is returning tomorrow," he said when Edward met him in the living room. "That will make meeting her at the house problematic, but I suggested I could take her to town on her day off and show her the sights. She seemed quite pleased at the prospect."

"That's great, Brent. When does Paula get off?"

"She has every Thursday off."

"You can take her in Davy, of course."

"Thank you, sir."

"You know, when you take her to town, walk along the sidewalk by the shops there, looking in the windows. It's called *window shopping*. If she sees something she likes and remarks on it, that would be a good opportunity to buy her a gift."

"An excellent idea, sir. I also want to take her through the park and to see the town history museum, just as you took Cindy when she visited last year."

"Good idea. That reminds me, Brent, I need to contact Cindy and see what's up with her employer and her next time off."

"Indeed sir, you should keep your romance active."

"Ha! Now *you're* giving the love advice!"

The following Thursday, Brent borrowed Davy and took Paula to town. Paula was wearing a day dress and sensible brown walking shoes that Victoria had purchased for her for when Paula accompanied her on shopping trips. After visiting the town museum, they walked through the park and past some shop windows. Paula saw a small silver bracelet in a store window and remarked on its beauty. Brent entered the store with Paula and purchased the trinket. He fastened it on her wrist and Paula wore it proudly. "I thank you, Mr. Brent. I won't wear it when I work, of course," she said, "but only when I go out with you. I have a cubby and a shelf in the pantry that Miss Victoria has given to me in which to keep my things."

"How was your trip to town?" asked Edward when Brent returned later that day.

"It was marvelous. I took your advice and went window shopping with Miss Paula. She liked a silver bracelet and I bought it for her. I think I am progressing in the wooing. She thanked me again after I walked her to her door."

"Did she give you a kiss?"

"No, and we are both of the soft lipped variety of robot,[5] so we will have to try that at some point."

---

[5] Brent and Paula are both able to form words with lips and tongue much as humans do, rather than using an electro-acoustic speaker in their mouths as in some of the less costly robots.

"So, what's the next step in your courtship strategy?"

"Well, sir, you wrote poetry to Cindy, and that seemed to work, at least in the long term. After all, you were talking about creating children when you saw her in Hawai'i. So, I think I will write a sonnet for her."

"Sounds good. I'd like to see it before you show it to her. Just to make sure, okay?"

"Yes, sir, I will be happy to have you review it."

The next day Brent printed his poem and handed it to Edward, and then Brent recited it:

Being the Kiss

When the evening star is as bright as this

Some people wonder and others believe

So much they become less able to see

An opportunity too good to miss

Who in not of miss out as not above

Projecting their own image on the sky

Given to open themselves to receive

Like a pelican presenting its bill

Paying by praying for what is for free

Feeling holier than some about it

As I am one of the some to wonder

And it could be just me but I doubt it

When the evening star is as bright as this

> Some people and one of them might be me
>
> Feel a sense of universality
>
> As if the universe offers a kiss
>
> As free as we were always meant to be
>
> Not above of but in with and under
>
> To love and to know if not to know why
>
> And if some people will not be I will
>
> An opportunity too good to miss
>
> By seeing the light and hearing the call
>
> Of the universe as the call of love
>
> By being at one with the one in all
>
> Giving receiving and being the kiss
>
> When the evening star is as bright as this[6]

When he was done reciting the sonnet, Edward said, "That's quite good, Brent. A lot better than I could do."

"Thank you, sir. I am going to recite it to her the next chance I get."

"And I assume you know that Venus is currently the evening star."

"Yes, and I will show that to her as well."

"It sounds to me like you have your courtship process well in hand."

---

[6] By Steven Curtis Lance, written in 2010, used with permission.

"Thank you, sir. Now I will shine my shoes, and yours as well." Brent put away the paper with the poem and went about his work.

The next Thursday afternoon, Brent met Paula at Victoria's house and showed her the poem and recited it to her. She said, "That is lovely, Mr. Brent. May I keep the paper? I will put it with my things in the pantry."

"Of course, my dear Miss Paula. I wrote it for *you*."

Then Brent told Paula about Venus being visible at sundown. Having borrowed Davy again, Brent took Paula to a lovers' lookout on a nearby hill and they watched the setting sun together. Then, as the sky grew darker, Brent pointed out the evening star, and said, "Look Paula, that is the goddess of love, and it shines brightly before any other stars are visible in the sky. The moon will be rising behind us in a few minutes, and we can stay and watch that too."

"I see what you mean in the poem by 'as bright as this.' It is quite lovely."

They lingered long enough to see the moonrise, and then Brent took Paula home. On the doorstep of Victoria's house, she gave him a kiss.

Robot Domesticity

Ah! There is nothing like staying at home, for real comfort.

—Jane Austen

On a summer morning, after a shopping trip to town, Brent and Edward were unloading groceries from Davy and carrying them into the house. Davy had parked near the kitchen door and after the groceries were unloaded, he drove to his carport with the photovoltaic solar panel roof and plugged himself into the charging outlet. As Brent and Edward were together in the kitchen putting away their purchases, Brent asked Edward, "How is your reading of Jack London going?"

"I read his presumably autobiographical *Martin Eden* some time ago and I've just finished his masterpiece novel *The Valley of the Moon*. Those books reveal a lot about London himself. The main characters are modeled on people close to him. If the parallel holds true, both Herbert Spencer and Frederich Nietzsche strongly influenced London. But those two philosophers were at odds with each other. Nietzsche disagreed with Darwinism and believed Spencer to be decadent."

"Very interesting, sir."

"Yes, Brent, and Jack London was able somehow to reconcile the competing philosophies. London's character in the first book, *Martin Eden*, even referred to himself as one of Nietzsche's 'blond beasts,' an amoral man whose strength justified his taking what he wanted."

Brent replied, "Spencer was a professional philosopher who had a great following among his peers. Nietzsche's thought seems to me to be more like a bundle of opinions than any coherent philosophy."

Edward said. "Nietzsche considered Spencer to be decadent because of Spencer's belief in the importance of altruism in ethics—such decadence would, in Nietzsche's mind, inhibit the flourishing of humanity. He was really hard over on that."

Brent added, "Anti-egalitarianism is as old as the neolithic tribes with their chiefs, spiritual leaders, and other privileged persons. I would hardly call Nietzsche's approach innovative."

"That's true, Brent, but it can be argued that those exalted persons in ancient societies paid their way with effective leadership and added cultural value. Until they stepped over the line into tyranny, of course."

"If the novel is any indication," Brent said, "Jack London was generous with his friends. Martin Eden repaid any kindness a hundred times over."

"True, Brent. Quite true. And it's interesting to note that Nietzsche was an influence on writers and politicians throughout the century that followed. Adolf Hitler, Ayn Rand, and Anton LaVey[7] all show evidence of the *mark of the beast*, so to speak."

---

[7] Anton LaVey was the founder of the Church of Satan and author of *The Satanic Bible*.

Having finished putting the groceries away, Brent said, "Miss Paula is coming over to help me with cleaning the floors. Miss Victoria gave her permission."

"Good. I think it's nice that you two are spending productive time together. I will install another wall charger so you both can trickle charge together when work is completed."

* * *

Cindy had attended her spycraft course with great interest. She particularly liked the sessions on counter-surveillance. She felt that the techniques could be useful in her infiltration. During the times that she would need to report back her status, she would need to be sure that she was not under surveillance herself. One of the exercises she enjoyed was tailing and evading a tail. Students were paired off and taken to a business district in the city. One student of each pair was to detect a person following (the tail) and try to lose the tail. The tail would try to avoid being detected and to stay with the subject.

During the exercise, when Cindy was the subject to be followed, she used an old trick to detect the tail. Walking along the street, every time she looked around she saw no one who looked like a tail. She went up to a store window and pretended to examine the wares inside but was able to see the street in the reflection of the glass. She waited, looking, and then she saw her tail, farther away and across the street, step out of the shadow of a doorway, move toward her, and then duck back into another doorway. She made a mental note of the tail's appearance and clothing.

Now that she knew where the tail was, she formed a plan. She walked on, then stopped and stood still as if she had forgotten something. Then she turned and moved quickly into a store. She went through the store and out the back door and over to the pub next door. Using the pub's rear entrance, she sought the restroom and hid there for a few minutes. Then she looked out the restroom door into the pub. Not seeing her tail, she walked to the front of the pub and looked out the window. Still not seeing her tail, she took a seat at a table and waited ten minutes.

Cindy exited the pub through the front door and, before stepping into the sunlight, she looked up and down the street carefully before continuing to her destination, a simulated dead drop. Having lost Cindy, her tail did not arrive, and Cindy was rewarded with a good score for the exercise.

The next day, Mr. Simpson briefed them for their final exercise in evading surveillance. "It is absolutely imperative that if you are not certain you are unobserved that you not approach a dead drop. A dead drop only works as a communication resource if the opposition is unaware of it. The minute the dead drop is compromised it must be abandoned. Therefore, if you have any suspicion that you are being tailed, you must not go near a dead drop. For this exercise, you will work in pairs, two on one side heading to a dead drop and two opposition tailing the first pair.

"If there is only one tail, then two agents working together make it easier to detect and evade the tail. However, when the opposition is also working in pairs, it can become rather difficult, as you will see. If the security of a dead drop operation cannot be ascertained after a specified time, have a rendezvous point where you can meet to confirm an abort."

Cindy and Sarah were paired for this exercise to get to a dead drop location unobserved. Cindy started out and Sarah followed at a good distance, watching her back. When Sarah saw an opposition tail follow Cindy, she headed for a rendezvous point where she could tell Cindy to abort the dead drop run.

* * *

The summer days grew warmer. Edward kept in shape by playing tennis in the morning and swimming in the afternoon. Sometimes he would play tennis against Brent. Sometimes friends would come by to play. Paula came over from time to time to assist Brent, and sometimes he would cross the street to be with Paula. Now and then they rode together in Davy or in Victoria's car for joint shopping trips.

After the second inductive charger had been installed in his living room, Edward was not surprised one day to see Brent and Paula standing at the wall holding hands, both completely motionless.

* * *

One day, having finished his mid-morning chores, Brent was standing alone at the inductive wall charger. Edward came into the living room. "Have you seen my book?"

"It's on the corner table, by the window, sir."

"Thank you, Brent." Edward walked over and picked up his antique copy of Ernest Hemingway's *To Have and Have Not*. He sat down in an armchair across the room from Brent and opened the book. "These Hemingway novels are fairly quick reads. I'm enjoying this one."

"Indeed, sir, his nonfiction books like *Death in the Afternoon* and *A Moveable Feast* are somewhat longer."

Continuing his pause before reading, Edward said, "I had no idea that fuel for fishing boats back then was so expensive!" He found his place in the book and began to read After a while, he put the book down and said, "How's your love life, Brent?"

"I am glad you asked, sir. Paula and I are doing tremendously well."

"That's good to hear."

"And I am sorry you have not heard from Cindy for a while. I understand she last said she was going on an undercover mission."

"That's right, and I have no idea when she will return. I miss her. I worry about her, too."

"When she returns from her mission, I understand you two will begin to plan your wedding."

"Yes, I have that to look forward to."

"You know, sir, you could be planning your wedding now instead of waiting."

"No, Brent, that wouldn't work. Part of the joy of wedding planning is doing it together."

"Please tell me about marriage, sir."

"Sure." Edward thought for a moment, then said, "When two people are drawn together by a mutual desire for affection and companionship, and possibly reproduction, they can agree to get married. The government sanctions marriages, giving special protections to married people and any children they might produce. Marriages are intended to last a long time, often for life, but there are provisions for dissolving marriages when mutually desirable. Or in some cases, one person can break out of a marriage if needed. Does that help?"

"Yes, sir, it does. You have given a good summation. Do you think marriages of robots will ever be sanctioned?"

"I suppose that remains to be seen. Are you thinking of marriage? You haven't known Paula very long, you know. Conventional wisdom is that the best marriages come only after several months of courtship or longer."

"The thought has occurred to me, sir, but I do not think our relationship has yet advanced to that stage. It merely passed through my mind when we were talking about your upcoming wedding."

"I see, Brent, but if your marriage were to come to pass, it would probably be another first for robots."

"Indeed, sir, it may be."

* * *

Brent continued to visit Paula across the road from time to time. Victoria didn't mind as Brent often gave Paula pointers that helped her with her domestic service. Paula reciprocated by visiting and assisting Brent when needed, and Brent continued to take Paula out on her days off.

Edward observed all this with curiosity but he maintained his detachment. He wondered where it could be going. Would it, like most romances, play itself out or would it lead to something longer lasting?

Fun for All

The highest activity a human being can attain is learning for understanding, because to understand is to be free.

—Baruch Spinoza

After spending a pleasant morning sipping coffee and perusing the news at the Coffee Corner in town, Edward returned home well before lunchtime. Davy dropped him off at the front walkway and went to park himself at the solar-roofed parking shelter in the rear. As he approached the house, Edward could hear the pop-popping of a tennis ball, so he took the side walkway around back and over to the tennis court. Brent and Paula were playing tennis.

Edward approached the court and watched. A lengthy baseline rally was underway. Finally, Brent sent a hard drive and pressed his advantage, winning the point.

Edward said, "Good one!"

"Thank you, sir," replied Brent as he and Paula walked toward Edward, then standing by a net post. "Victoria went into town for a meeting and gave Paula the morning off. I thought I would teach her how to play tennis."

"You seem to have taught her well, Brent. I see you got her some tennis things, too."

"Yes, on one of my trips to town I bought her some tennis clothes, shoes, and a racket, intending to teach her should the occasion arise."

Paula said, "Brent is so nice to me. I love him!" She was wearing the silver bracelet that Brent had bought her earlier.

"I can see you are both in love," said Edward. The popping sound resumed as he walked to the house.

* * *

After finishing her spycraft course, Cindy flew to the London offices of Smith, Pearson, and Smith, Ltd., to meet with Mr. Scott for her final briefing before beginning her undercover assignment. After exchanging pleasantries, Mr. Scott said, "We have prepared an undercover identity for you. You will be Jane Cushion, MFA, an art historian. You will have just arrived in Kansas City. That will explain the lack of a circle of friends, and you will be looking for employment, possibly at a museum or college."

"I see."

"We will give you a false personal device that will have all your identification data and some dummy photos, messages, and so on, that will support your new persona. Now, normally, a false personal device is illegal for civilians, but as this undercover operation is sponsored by the SSA, you are covered as a secret agent on an authorized mission."

"I understand."

"And as I mentioned earlier, this is a surveillance mission. We do not expect you to make any arrests, but merely to report your findings on a regular basis. We don't expect any danger, and therefore you will not be armed. Should danger become apparent, you will be recalled from the mission. Clear?"

"Clear."

"We have scouted the area and set up several drop boxes in public yet secluded areas for communication on a regular schedule with backups, as you were taught in spy school. You will have a supply of micro-mems to which your personal device can write, avoiding network communications. Naturally, you will not know nor ever see your corresponding agent. Now, let's go down to the equipment lab and get you outfitted. You will have an appropriate wardrobe, reference works, and so on."

* * *

One late-summer afternoon, Brent was standing at his wall charger in the living room, thinking. While he knew that he was an artificial being, he considered himself to be alive, not in the organic sense, but in the practical. Brent was puzzled. He wanted to know if the *fact* of life, such as one finds it, had an overarching meaning. Life in the particular, such as his own life, and life in general, relating to the origin of life, the history of evolution, and where it was going. He had good reason to believe it was a problem of great import. Philosophers called the field exploring the associated questions "eschatology."

Edward was sitting in an armchair across the room from him, reading an ancient novel, *Pride and Prejudice*, and, when Edward turned a page, Brent interrupted him. "Sorry to disturb you, sir. A question has occurred to me."

Edward placed a bookmark and looked up at Brent, who remained standing at the wall. "That's alright, Brent. What's your question?"

"Do you remember when we were in Hawai'i and we heard about a professor there who used to teach a course at the university called 'The Meaning of Existence'?"

"Yes, I recall that. I think he was a mentor to the governor that the spaceport there was named for."

"That's right. Do you know if he ever defined that meaning, or was it just a teaser to draw students to his class?"

Edward looked up at the ceiling and thought for a few seconds. "Now that you bring it up, I think not. He didn't declare that life had meaning, much less definitize what it might be."

"Thank you, Edward. Your opinion is congruent to mine. It is not often that a philosopher will go out on a limb and make a statement that he cannot prove with certainty."

Edward said, "He probably used the question as a jumping-off point for group discussions or writing assignments." Edward picked up his book. "I'm sure you're going to research this some more."

"Quite right, sir. Does this have any relation to your theories on hedonism, sir?"

"No, Brent. The question of meaning and purpose may be orthogonal to ethical considerations of living an upright life. However, that's an intriguing thought. What if the meaning of existence is aligned with the ethics of right action? Hmm. Now that I think about it, perhaps a coherent ethics may depend on a correct theory of existence." Edward paused a minute, gazed at the ceiling, then opened his book and resumed reading.

A few days later, Edward was sitting out in the shade of the gazebo he had earlier designed and built. He was again reading an old fashioned paper book, *Great Expectations*, having finished *Pride and Prejudice*, when Brent, wearing his valet uniform with bowler hat, brought him an iced tea on a silver salver. He put the glass down on the table next to Edward and took a couple of steps back.

"Thank you, Brent."

"You are most welcome, sir."

When Brent remained standing in front of him, Edward asked, "What is it, Brent?"

"Do you recall, sir, when we were musing a few days ago on the content of Professor Mitsuo Aoki's course on the meaning of existence?"

"I sure do. I'm still puzzled. What did you find out?"

"Well sir, it is complicated. First, existence is experienced by every conscious entity."

"True."

"Second, beings like me, who do not fit the normal definition of living, have conscious existence, and further, many organic living things like plants do not have consciousness. So, to simplify, I am collapsing or merging the concepts of life and existence, such that the term *meaning of life* applies to all life and conscious machines as one aggregate."

Edward took a sip of his tea. "Fair enough. I don't think you can go too far wrong, at least for an initial attack. So, then, for our purposes, the meaning of life and the meaning of existence would be the same thing."

"Indeed, sir, a useful simplification that sacrifices nothing of importance."

"So, Brent, cutting to the chase, I suppose you found that there are two schools of thought on this. One that claims life has meaning and one that claims it has none?"

"Well, sir, it is in fact more complicated than that. One opinion is that life has no meaning, but it has a purpose. This has been described as an imperative for genetic or memetic replication, a drive to reproduce, which is a purpose without further meaning."

"I see. Purely mechanistic."

"Yes, sir. Another view, the majority religious one, is that both meaning and purpose are predefined for us by supernatural sources accessible to a few by mysterious means."

"Yes, Brent, those are well known, but they are hardly to be considered philosophy."

"Indeed, sir. Love of wisdom implies being able to change one's mind with new facts, and religious people are notorious for being unamenable to new ideas."

"What else?"

"And lastly, sir, is the nihilist school, which believes that life or existence has neither meaning nor purpose. The titular character in Shakespeare's Scottish play described this condition as being 'full of sound and fury, signifying nothing.'"

"Ah, yes, the question occurs in literature. I seem to recall that in one fictional book series, the answer to the question of 'life, the universe, and everything' was forty-two."

"Very droll, sir."

Edward took another sip of his tea. "I suppose, Brent, that you have formulated your own answer to this question. What *is* the meaning of life?"

"Sir, it remains complicated, but the answer requires defining two viewpoints, that of the collective, and that of the individual. Any answer must satisfy both. The *purpose* of life is to achieve individual and collective prosperity, and the *meaning* of life is in the enjoyment of the successes of oneself and others."

Edward drained his glass and put it down. "That's a little long winded, but simple enough, I suppose. I can't argue with it. Maybe shorten it to *fun for all*." He picked up his book.

Brent said, "That sums it up nicely. Thank you, sir." He took Edward's empty glass, put it on the tray, and carried it back into the house.

Abstraction Arguments

There is a transcendental dimension beyond language. It's just hard as hell to talk about it.

—Terence McKenna

Brent and Edward were returning from the modern art museum in the big city after seeing a one-woman abstract show there. Aircar Maxine was unusually chatty on the twenty minute flight home. She had parked in an aircar parking tower slot next to a flying car named Tert, and he must have stimulated her conversational inclination. Brent and Edward watched the cumulus clouds below seeming to creep along as seen from their altitude. They approached the vicinity of their demesne and in their descent to the household landing pad, Maxine let herself drop rapidly before increasing power dramatically for a smooth and precise touchdown.

Upon landing, as Maxine's twin transverse-mounted and opposed hydrogen turbines spun down, Edward said, "Maxine, that near free-fall descent was too thrilling for my taste. In the future, please keep your vertical acceleration above half a gee."

"Yes, sir. Tert told me that his child passengers enjoy rapid descents, so I thought I would try it."

"If I should ever have children, I will rethink my policy."

"Yes, sir," Maxine opened her doors and Brent and Edward stepped out.

Brent said, "It is good to be back on *terra firma*, sir."

Edward gazed through his tall pine trees to the road along the front of his rural house. All was quiet, no traffic in sight. "Yes, that was a fun excursion this morning, but it's good to be home. Let's go inside." He headed to the side door with Brent following and carrying their day bag.

After putting things away, Brent prepared lunch for Edward. After eating, Edward thanked Brent, who said, "The weather is cooling off. In a few months we will have icy sidewalks again."

"I don't want to think about it. Let's get through the winter holidays[8] first, and then perhaps we can plan a return trip to Hawai'i."

"We both enjoyed last winter's trip there, did we not, Edward?"

"Absolutely, and maybe this time we can see other islands than O'ahu."

"Indeed, sir, that is a possibility to pleasurably contemplate."

"Yes, we had some good times there, and between the beach and the passing showers, your solar umbrella became your *vaude mecum*."

"Yes, sir, I did carry it around there a lot."

"Your frequent shadings of me on the beach were welcome."

---

[8] Winter Solstice parties and New Year's celebrations.

* * *

Later that day, Edward was in the living room examining his collection of silver dimes and shillings from the 20th century. He was in the good light at a table near the rear French doors and he put down his magnifying glass as Brent approached him from behind.

"I thought I was walking quietly enough not to disturb you, sir."

"I sensed you by your effect on the ambient sound field in this room, Brent. Your body absorbs and reflects sound so that I knew someone was approaching. You know that feeling one sometimes gets that someone is behind them?"

"Yes, sir. I have learned something. Thank you, sir."

"What did you want to see me about, Brent?"

"Well, sir, it's about that abstract art exhibit at the museum today. I was wondering what you thought of it."

"That show featuring the artist Ergadser Ruddsnik?"

"Indeed, sir, it seems the artist has hit upon a radical departure from the current scene, as it were."

"I thought it was an interesting mix of unusual colors and forms leading to many suggestions of I don't know what."

"Neither do I, sir. It was, however, most certainly abstraction."

"Abstract: the word is from the Latin meaning 'to drag away from.' Abstracted from what, then?"

"Probably from those unconscious suggestions that *you* don't clearly understand."

"Yes, most likely, Brent. We'll probably have to go back and look at it again. Maybe the second time around the significance will be more apparent."

"Perhaps, sir."

Being a computer scientist by profession, Edward just had to add, "Abstraction is a concept that is quite useful in computer science, you now, but the application of that word to art is probably different."

Brent asked, "How so, sir?"

"The forms of abstraction useful to software engineers and computer scientists all involve simplification by eliminating unnecessary detail."

"It seems to me, sir, that abstract art does that. Classic representational art exults in realistic detail, whereas the modernists began to play with color and shapes in simpler forms. Cartoons drawn for children can be considered as abstractions as well."

Edward said, "Yes, Brent, I can see that. Simplification to help communicate something."

"As Einstein said, sir, a description ought to be 'as simple as possible, but no simpler.'"

"Yes, Brent, but I believe the descriptions to which he was referring were physical theories."

"Indeed so, sir."

"But appropriate simplifications can be tremendously useful. This reminds me of a story I heard as a student, told to my class in the university by a professor of computer science. It's a simple illustration of the utility of abstraction. It goes like this:

"Once upon a time there was a king who wanted his cartographers to make a new map of his kingdom. It was to be the best and most detailed map ever made. The cartographers went to work and produced a full scale map depicting every street, house, rock, tree, and blade of grass. The problem was that when the map was unfolded, it covered the entire kingdom. The lesson being, of course, that to be useful, a map must necessarily omit detail."

"Indeed sir, that is quite an illustrative story."

"I know you've never been there, Brent, but take for example the famous schematic map of the London Underground. That map is powerfully useful because it includes only the information required to navigate that transportation system."

"Indeed, sir, I have heard of that famous map."

"Yes, Brent, tube riders want to know how many stops there are to their destination and they don't really care about the exact distance or compass direction. That reminds me of another useful abstraction: numbers!"

"Yes, sir. Numbers are among the purest of abstractions. In some cases, only the number of sheep in a herd is needed, reducing a complicated physical situation to a single item."

"Right," said Edward. "Counting sheep led to pure mathematics and things like irrational and imaginary numbers."

Brent proceeded, "Recording numbers in clay and papyrus also led to generalized writing, an abstraction and preservation of language."

"Yes, and speaking and writing words, that is, symbols of extracted meaning, made your profession, philosophy, itself, possible."

"Indeed, sir, and that brings a whole new problem."

"How so, Brent?"

"Well, sir, this is something that Immanuel Kant wrote extensively about. Because our thoughts are symbols, and our writings about our thoughts are symbols, we never really deal with things in themselves. We can know only our perceptions of things. It's like all of philosophy is one step removed from reality."

Edward looked thoughtfully at the sweet gum trees through the windows for a minute. Then he said, "And being in touch with reality means everything to a philosopher. It must be like trying to feel the texture of wood while wearing mittens."

"Precisely, sir."

Edward picked up his magnifying glass. Brent went to get his feather duster. Edward instructed the sound system to play Bach's fifth Brandenburg Concerto. The sublime music swelled as he resumed examining his coins.

* * *

Cindy Fairfax flew to Kansas City from London on a ballistic passenger rocket. She had adopted her new identity as Jane Cushion, a teacher of art and art history. Born in the Midwest, her being partly educated in Britain explained her slight British accent. Her cover story was that being new in town, she was looking for a job and hadn't been having any luck with educational institutions, so she would settle for clerical/administrative work. Her application for employment to the Kansas City office of the Humans First movement took the form of a cover letter and résumé.

Wearing her red ball cap with the HF logo, Cindy took the lift to the fifteenth floor of a modest but new-looking building, headed to the Humans First office, and walked in. "I am Jane Cushion," she said to the receptionist. "I saw your advertisement of an open position in administration. May I leave my résumé?"

"Yes, that will be fine. We will contact you shortly."

Cindy thanked the receptionist and departed. The next day she was messaged to arrange for an interview appointment.

* * *

Brent was fishing leaves out of the swimming pool with a long handled sieve. He was wearing his khaki work clothes, rubber soled work boots, and a cloth hat to shade his eyes which did not have the polarized filters available with the latest model robots. He found that if he stood with his back to the sun, he could more easily see to the bottom to get the leaves. The sun was in the east so he was facing the house as he worked and was able to see Edward approaching.

"Oh, there you are," said Edward as he came to the pool deck. "Thanks for cleaning the pool."

"It's all part of the job, sir."

"And thanks again for that wonderful breakfast."

"Do not mention it, sir."

"But I do have a suggestion for improvement."

"Please tell me what it is."

"If you fry the eggs at a lower temperature they won't scorch."

"I see, sir. I thought you might like the light brown coloration of the fried egg."

"That's not necessary, Brent, and the scorched part has a metallic taste."

"I did not know that. I will endeavor to do better. I appreciate your help in my improvement efforts."

"Thank you, Brent." Edward looked around. The pool furniture was all clean and well placed. He hesitated a moment, then said, "By the way, Brent, I will be attending a software developer's conference in Kansas City next month. I'll be putting on a workshop on modeling human-robot interactions. You may use Davy to take Paula out while I'm gone, if you like."

"Thank you, sir."

Brent went back to his pool cleaning and Edward returned to the house.

* * *

Cindy, as Jane Cushion, was staying in an inexpensive hotel while looking for an apartment and a job. She wore her new clothes and looked the part of a teacher or professor. She wore her HF red hat again when she went back to the HF regional headquarters for her employment interview. She arrived at the HF office at the appointed time and was ushered into the office of regional leader Albert Humbert, who stood up from his chair behind his desk and said, "Please come in Ms Cushion. Have a seat," and indicated a chair near his desk.

"Thank you, Mr. Humbert." Cindy sat down and Mr. Humbert sat.

"You have an impressive résumé. I see you have an MFA in Art History and you have some experience teaching."

"That's right."

"I understand that teaching positions are scarce right now."

"Yes, I've been looking."

"And you have some experience in clerical work and sales."

"Yes, when I was in school in London."

"Sales work shows you are good meeting with the public and can be trusted with monetary transactions."

"I like to think so."

"Why did you come to Kansas City, Ms. Cushion?"

"A friend recommended it for the friendly people and positive culture. She said there was also work in teaching and curating, but that hasn't panned out."

"I see. There is just one little item that I would like to clear up. You know we are a political organization, and we need to know if your beliefs are of the right character. I see you are wearing an HF hat, but we need to be sure. Now, it says here you were arrested at an anti-robot personhood rally not too long ago."

"Yes, sir. Some bad actors started throwing things and it got out of hand. I was only holding a sign, but the police rounded all of us up."

"That is quite understandable, Ms. Cushion. I have been in some altercations myself when I was younger."

"I have avoided activism since then," said Cindy.

"Well, we are looking for someone to fill an administrative role with a pathway to management. With your education and experience, I think you might be a good fit. Would you like to give it a try?"

"Indeed, sir, yes, I would. Thank you Mr. Humbert."

"Can you start next Monday morning? At nine o'clock?"

"Yes, sir, I will be here then."

Panpsychism

Panpsychism is sometimes dismissed as a crazy view, but this reaction on its own is not a serious objection. While the view is counterintuitive to some, there is good reason to think that any view of consciousness must embrace some counterintuitive conclusions.

—David Chalmers

Edward had just finished his light breakfast of toast and marmalade and was sipping his second cup of coffee when Brent came over to the breakfast table to remove the plate. "I trust you slept well last night, sir."

"Yes, Brent, quite well, thank you. Cindy sent me a message that she is on her undercover assignment. She can't tell me where it is but she says it's not all that far from here. Within a couple of thousand kilometers, I suppose."

"I suppose, sir, that if you travel and bump into her, you should pretend not to recognize her."

"That's right. I don't want to blow her cover like I might have done running into her on the beach in Waikīkī last winter."

"Indeed, sir. Did she give any indication how long her assignment might last?"

"No, she didn't. How did you fare last night, standing at your wall charger and thinking?"

His breakfast duties completed, Brent switched from valet into personal friend mode. "Well, Edward, do you recall our past discussion about my eventually realizing I have been conscious all along and didn't know it?"

"I do. Yes, that was decidedly interesting."

"I said that I had been like a fish unaware of the water it swims in."

"I remember. Robot consciousness must be much more subtle than the human kind. We are often painfully aware of our qualia. We sometimes even get self-conscious in new situations, like when asked to speak in public."

"Yes, Edward. So, the thought occurred to me that there really is no explanation of *how* consciousness arises. It is the old so-called 'easy' problem of consciousness. The 'hard' one being *why*."

"Yes, Brent, the old mind-brain duality. An old and very hard problem in philosophy."

"That is correct. Well, last night I began to reflect on some older philosophies, such as those of Spinoza and Berkeley that invoked a concept of panpsychism to explain consciousness."

"Right. I have heard of that but never gave it much thought. But I can see how everything being conscious from atoms on up would turn that dualism into monism. I assume that is your desired result?"

At this point, probably due to philosophical excitement, Brent started getting exceedingly informal. "Darn tootin' Eddy. Conceiving dualism boggles the mind to no end. Monism, or the universe being all one substance, rests easier on the brain processors."

"Okay, so problem solved!"

"Not so fast, Eddy. In humans and intelligent animals, consciousness seems to be related to specific electro-chemical processes. Such states do not exist in robotic brains, which are all transistorized."

"I see, I think. So, under the monism of panpsychism, any transistorized object, such as my personal device, would be conscious?

"That's right, but in a rather rudimentary way. We could never know if it were so."

Edward paused a moment, deep in thought, then said, "Yes, Brent, panpsychism raises the further difficulty of explaining why most of human minds are unconscious, as Freud and Jung described."

As the philosophical tension subsided, Brent began to revert to his valet mode. "You have put your finger on it, sir. Panpsychism is, therefore, seriously flawed as a theory of consciousness."

"I agree, Brent."

"And if you don't mind, sir, I will dust and polish the living room tables this morning."

"Dust away, Brent, dust away."

* * *

Cindy returned to her hotel room and followed up on some leads in her search for an apartment. She contracted for a furnished one bedroom month-to-month on the 44th floor of a high-rise downtown. She moved in the next day. She looked around the place and, finding it clean and satisfactory, she made a shopping list. After lunch in a café on the ground floor, she went shopping for household supplies. She purchased bath towels, linens, tableware, cooking utensils, and many other things she needed to turn her apartment into a cozy home. That evening, she drew back the curtain in the living room and admired the sunset in her view to the west.

The sunset reminded her of the time when she had first arrived at Edward's house after their trip to Mars. Brent had urged them to sit outside and brought them glasses and a bottle of wine to sip as they watched the sun go down. The memory gave her a nostalgic feeling. *I miss Edward*, she thought. She sat at the small desk and, using her personal device, prepared a status report for Mr. Scott. She then encrypted the report onto one of the rice grain sized mini-mems for later deposit in a secret drop box.

* * *

After Brent completed his morning chores he prepared lunch of a sandwich and fresh cherries, which Edward ate with relish. Brent removed the sandwich plate with the cherry pits and the empty cherry bowl as Edward drained his iced tea glass. Edward said, "It seems to me, Brent, that your romance with Paula is progressing well. Have you thought about where it might be going?"

"Well, sir, I suppose the human analog would be engagement, marriage, and child rearing."

"If your romance should lead to marriage, you may very well be the first two robots in history to get married. It would be yet another first for you, Brent."

"Indeed, sir, but Paula would need to apply for and be granted personhood before we could get married."

"And I'm sure you know that robots can't have children. It's in regard to what we call knowledge of *the birds and the bees.*"

"Yes, sir, but Paula and I could adopt human orphans. We have even discussed it."

"Yes, Brent, as legal persons you probably will be allowed to adopt babies. I bet robots would be darned good at child rearing."

"Indeed, sir. Paula and I have been researching the subject. We might even be said to possess the knowledge equivalent of a bachelor's degree in education."

"Let's not get the cart ahead of the horse, now Brent. First you have to determine if your relationship warrants marriage."

"Yes, sir, you are right as usual, and I appreciate your obscure transportation reference."

* * *

Cindy arrived at the fifteenth floor offices of the regional directorship of Humans First, Inc., at nine in the morning on Monday,

85

right on time. Mr. Humbert greeted her, introduced her to her coworkers and showed her to her shared office. She asked some questions of Mr. Humbert to clarify her duties and then set to work. She had been given basic access to the information system which she began to explore.

The days went by and Cindy made friends with her coworkers. She went to lunch from time to time with Beth who shared her office with her. She and Beth were responsible for coordinating outreach events in the region. Cindy became adept at her duties and she was given more responsibility, and higher access levels in the computer system.

* * *

One day at lunch time, Cindy went to a fast food joint and bought a tofu burger and iced tea to go. She went to a nearby park and found a bench in the shade and began to eat. She ate half the burger and drank the iced tea. Then she carried the paper sack with the rubbish to a park restroom, went into a stall, and sat down. She inserted three mini-mems into the remaining half of the tofu patty. She took the rubbish bag and made a roundabout journey to the rubbish bin that had been identified as a drop box. Verifying she was not followed, she dropped the rubbish sack in the bin and walked back to work.

A few minutes later, an SPS agent, appearing to be a homeless person, came by and rummaged in the bin, finally removing the sack Cindy had left. He moved on and disappeared from sight.

* * *

Another day, Cindy went to lunch with Beth, who said, "The job doesn't pay that well, but it's good to be making a difference. Humans First is helping to guide government priorities and educate the public."

In character as Jane Cushion, Cindy replied, "That's right. As our leaders say, God created man to be above his own creations."

"Yes, those godless atheists, both human and robot, need to be taught their place in the world."

As the weeks went by, Cindy was able to delve deeper into the computer systems of the regional office. The system security wasn't what it ought to have been. Cindy was able to access history files and erase traces of her activities in the databases. Using the forensic accounting techniques she had developed earlier, she found evidence of illegal fundraising practices and ties to organized crime. She could download data to her personal device and periodically sent full reports to Mr. Scott, encrypting mini-mems in her apartment after work, and routinely depositing them in different drop boxes following a memorized schedule.

* * *

After her second month of employment, Mr. Humbert called Cindy into his office for a consultation. As she sat in the chair indicated, Mr. Humbert said, "I have heard nothing but good things about your work here, Ms. Cushion. How are you liking your assignments?"

"The work has been interesting, so far, and I like my coworkers."

"That's good. You know I have added to your responsibilities and elevated your system access accordingly."

"Thank you, sir."

Mr. Humbert said, "Now I have something else you might find interesting. It will not be dangerous. I guarantee it."

"Oh, what is it?"

"The Solar System Computer Society is having its annual autonomous systems conference next week, here in Kansas City. We would like you to infiltrate that conference. You are fairly new in town, but we will give you an alias, just in case. We will pay your registration fee and arrange a hotel room for you and cover other expenses. All you have to do is to go to various sessions and socialize with the attendees and keep your eyes and ears open. We will expect a report of your observations, of course."

"That sounds interesting."

"The conference begins Monday after next and ends the following Saturday. Pay particular attention to any developments of deceptive practices in robotics."

"I will, Mr. Humbert. I will."

"We will give you a new personal device with a fake identity for you. You can pick a name you like. That will allow you to register incognito."

"Isn't that illegal?"

"It's the only way for you to infiltrate without arousing suspicion. Besides, you're very unlikely to get caught, and if you do, you can say I told you it was accepted practice in industrial espionage."

"Well, okay. It should be interesting."

"That's the spirit!"

Robotics Conference

In a strange, foreign, far away land–how to enjoy yourself? How to eat well? What to do? How to do it? Rule one: get the hell away from the hotel as quickly as possible.

—Anthony Bourdain

Brent and Paula's romance flourished, with frequent visits and occasional outings. They talked about personhood for *her*, possible marriage, and maybe even looking into adopting human babies. They had ruled out attempting to design their own children. Only human babies could grow, and it would be cruel to produce small robots that couldn't grow up. Sure, it might be fun for a child robot to be a Peter Pan, for a while. It would not be good for the long term. It would have to be creating full sized robots or adopting human babies if they wanted a family of their own.

Paula broached the idea of personhood for herself to Victoria and the possibility of marriage. She also mentioned adoption. Victoria said, "No doubt a case can be made that robot persons have a legal right to adopt. However, adopting and rearing human children should be done only after the most careful consideration and consultation." Victoria said she would immediately represent Paula in her quest for personhood, much as she had done for Brent. She would first help Paula set up banking arrangements so that Paula could be paid a salary and then buy her freedom, as she had arranged for Brent to do. Victoria would voluntarily switch to an employee model for Paula from the current slavery one because it was the *right thing to do* in light of Paula's expressed wishes. She said, "An honorable person will not knowingly do anything that is unethical or fail to do the proper thing."

Paula said, "I thank you with profound gratitude, madam."

"I will write up your petition for personhood the next time I go to my office in town."

* * *

Cindy as Jane Cushion as Juanita Couch took a taxi on Monday to the grand hotel where the conference was being held. First she checked into the hotel with her new Juanita Couch ID and credit line. She went up to her room and unpacked her bag. Then she took the lift down to the lobby and registered for the conference with her new name and faux sponsoring company without any problems. She took her conference packet, in a handy carry bag, and went to an armchair in the lobby to read the conference schedule and plan which sessions she would attend. She wanted to maximize the likelihood of running into a developer of deceptive systems. That would be sure to please her employer, Mr. Humbert, one layer of deception upward. The irony wasn't lost on her.

As she looked at the conference events for the week, her eye caught "Workshop on Modeling Human-Robot Cooperative Federations," and then she saw the presenter, Edward Collier. *This will be interesting*, she thought. She looked up, and there, standing across the lobby, looking at his own copy of the program, was Edward himself.

Cindy stood up and walked over to Edward. As she approached, he looked up at her and she said, "Hello, my name is Juanita. Are you Edward?"

Catching on quickly to the undercover play-acting, and aware of the need to play along, Edward said, "Why, yes, I am. Pleased to meet you Juanita." They shook hands.

Cindy said, "I see you will be presenting the modeling workshop on Wednesday. I think I will attend."

"That will be nice. I think you will like it. I have several interesting speakers lined up."

"Very good. See you then."

"See you," said Edward.

Cindy went back to her armchair, glad that Edward played along, defusing a potential embarrassment to her mission. Having marked her program to indicate the sessions she wished to attend, Cindy put it back in the carry bag and took it upstairs to her room. Then she went out on the street, walking around and looking for suitable cafés and bistros for later consideration. The hotel's neighborhood was loaded with likely eating places, and she made many mental notes as she passed.

Cindy walked along the sidewalk, looking at the storefronts. Out of new habit acquired at spy school, she paused at a store window, looking at the reflection in the glass to see if she were being followed. She was not. *It's a relief*, she thought, *to have met with Edward early*. If the encounter had happened later with lots of people around, he might have blurted out "Hi, Cindy!" It might have come to nothing, but this was her first undercover assignment for Humans First, and it was just possible that they had sent someone to keep an eye on her.

When Cindy got back to the hotel, Edward was not in the lobby. She took a seat where she could watch the front door and pretended to read her program.

* * *

Having registered and gone back to his room, Edward wondered how he could contact Cindy without blowing her cover. He wasn't aware of the double layer of deception but he knew from her introduction that she was on an undercover mission. *Infiltrating a robotics conference?* He wondered why. *She likely has false credentials from a robotics company or university research lab*, he thought. *I guess I'll just play it by ear and see how it goes. This should be interesting. I hope there's no danger.*

Edward was becoming hungry. He didn't want to eat in the hotel restaurant so he went down to the lobby and out the front door to see if he could find a café or bistro on the street. Cindy watched from behind her program, then stood up and, keeping a moderate distance, followed Edward. Her recent training came in handy. When Edward stopped to look at a restaurant, she stopped too and pretended to window shop. After Edward had gotten a few blocks away from the hotel, Cindy approached him. "Hello, Edward. Remember me? I'm Juanita."

"Oh, hi Juanita. I was just looking for a place to eat lunch."

"I know a nice looking place just around that corner. Will you join me?"

93

"I would love to. Let's go."

Cindy led the way past an old brick building, and into a small restaurant. The place was busy, but the hostess led them to a small wooden table in a dark corner, near the kitchen door. They sat, and the hostess left two menus. The table was a little sticky, but otherwise clean. There were ferns in hanging baskets and cinema posters on the walls.

They decided to split a submarine sandwich. A waitress came and took their order, iced tea for Edward and lemonade for Cindy. The waitress brought the drinks quickly and as they waited for their food order to be filled, Cindy explained, "Of course you understand, Edward, that what I say here is confidential and not to be repeated anywhere." Cindy and Edward had complete trust in each other.

Edward looked around. Nobody was paying any attention to them, and the kitchen noises were likely to interfere with any eavesdropping, anyway. "Understood."

"My London employer has sent me here to infiltrate the regional headquarters of Humans First. They gave me the cover name of Jane Cushion, and I have rented a flat in that name here in this city. Coincidentally, Mr. Humbert of HF has sent me to infiltrate the robotics convention and is putting me up in the hotel under the cover name Juanita Couch. You must call me 'Juanita' if we should bump into each other later."

Edward said, "I see. Ironic as heck and it sure is coincidental us both landing in the same hotel."

"Yes, if this were a novel, nobody would believe it. I am supposed to keep an eye out for evidence of developers teaching robots deceptive practices. You know how paranoid the humans firsters are."

Cindy fell silent as the waitress approached with their sandwich, cut in half and presented on two plates with some chips. They began to eat with relish.

"Mmm, good sandwich," said Edward. "That name Humbert rings a bell. Wasn't he convicted of pedophilia some time back?"

"Possibly, but I suppose such a person would want to change his name once he paid his debt to society."

"You said you might attend my workshop on modeling of cooperation Wednesday morning, but I don't think anyone will be talking about deception."

"Yes, but I still plan to be there. I wouldn't miss it."

"For sure you will want to attend the session on 'Implementing Tact in Robot Communications.' My friend and coworker, Hadi, is putting it on." Edward pulled up the session on his personal device and showed it to Cindy. "It's on Tuesday, tomorrow afternoon."

"Tact?"

"Yes. Little white lies to save someone's feelings. It's a very tricky subject. One would think that robots should always be totally honest, but being tactful requires slight deceptions from time to time. It could become a slippery slope to compulsive lying. This may be what HF has in mind."

Cindy said, "I see. At least you developers are aware of the issue."

"Yes, it's a difficult problem. Brent, you know, seems to have developed tact on his own while keeping aware of the ethics of truth telling."

"Brent is tremendously precocious. Where is he, anyway?"

"I'm away for just a week, so I left him at home. You know, he's developed an infatuation with the robot maid, Paula, of Victoria's, so I gave him use of Davy to take her out on her days off."

"Amazing!"

"Yes, it will be interesting to see how it develops. Paula is thinking of pursuing legal personhood, like Brent."

They finished their food and drink and Cindy settled the bill. "Well, good luck to them both. Walk me back to the hotel?"

That evening, in her flat, Cindy filed two status reports. One to Mr. Scott using her Jane Cushion personal device and a shorter unencrypted one to Mr. Humbert from the Juanita Couch device.

* * *

On Tuesday morning, Brent messaged Victoria across the road.

I am taking Davy into town to get cleaning supplies. Perhaps Paula could come with me and do some shopping for you. Why make two trips?

Victoria was at work at her upstairs office when the message came in. She replied:

That's a good idea, Brent. How thoughtful of you. I will send Paula over now.

A few minutes later Paula arrived at the front door with shopping bags and a memorized list. Brent greeted her and invited her in while he got ready. He got his bowler and umbrella from his cupboard and said, "Ready? Let us go."

Davy was pulling up out front as they went out the front door. Davy opened the front curbside door and they got in. Paula slid across the bench seat to make room for Brent. Davy closed his door and began to roll. Paula said, "Thank you, Brent, for taking me to town."

"It is my pleasure, Paula. I have been thinking about the possibility of our marrying and adopting children."

"I have, too, Brent."

"I hope you are not disappointed when I say that perhaps we should slow down and not commit too quickly."

"No, Brent. I was thinking the same thing."

"Indeed? It occurred to me that baby humans probably deserve to be raised by real human parents. While robots can simulate humans to a great extent, there are organic considerations that are beyond robots' grasp."

"Those were my thoughts exactly. Neither of us has much experience with robot love and perhaps we should get better acquainted before a major commitment."

"I concur. Kiss me?"

Davy pulled up at the curb in front of the store and let out his passengers before going to park himself in the public structure.

* * *

Cindy attended Hadi's session on tact in robots, Edward's on modeling robot cooperation, and many others. In the discussion of tactfulness as a virtue in people and robots, she learned that total honesty can have negative consequences. In such situations, both people and robots are advised to say nothing by *tactfully* stepping around the issue. As Edward alluded earlier, such evasions can be a slippery slope to deliberate lying, so it remains an open issue. Cindy resolved to ask Brent about this issue later.

Opportunities for Cindy to meet surreptitiously with Edward were scarcer than a tolerant Red Hat. She did stand in line to talk to him after his modeling session and arranged for a dinner later, but they both knew the risk of being noticed together, so they minimized the times they spoke together in the hotel during the conference. Cindy told Edward she was not sure when she would be free of surveillance again and said for him to be patient. Edward understood and resigned himself to remaining in waiting mode. When the conference was over, Cindy went back to her rented flat in Kansas City and Edward flew back to his home.

Imprisonment

There is a stubbornness about me that never can bear to be frightened at the will of others. My courage always rises at every attempt to intimidate me.

—Jane Austen

When Maxine landed with Edward at his house late Sunday morning after the robotics conference in Kansas City, he walked to the kitchen door on the side of the house and let himself in. Brent, having finished his morning chores, was standing at his inductive wall charger in the living room, cogitating.

"What ho, Brent!"

"Welcome back, sir. Practicing your Shakespearian English?"

"I think it's more Wodehouse than Shakespeare. I just felt like being familiar today. I don't always need to be formal in our relations."

"How was the conference, sir?"

"Fine. My workshop was well received. You'll never guess who I ran into there."

"Well, sir, if I will never guess, you had better tell me."

"Cindy! She was on an undercover assignment so we had to be careful not to be seen together. It was frustrating and tantalizing.

We did get away for a lunch and a dinner but had to split up before returning to the hotel. We couldn't meet in our rooms because there was no telling who had access to internal hotel hallway surveillance. We met only in the lobby and conference rooms."

"You have my sympathy, sir."

"It was good to see her, but I can't help worrying about her on these missions."

* * *

Cindy went back to work at the HF regional headquarters on Monday after the robotics conference. She said good morning to the coworkers she passed on the way to her office. After checking her messages, she returned her Juanita Couch personal device to the administrative office. She got to keep the clothes she bought for the mission. She returned to her office, sat down at her desk, and began writing her full report on her surveillance work over the past week. The report was ready before close of business and she transmitted it to her boss, Mr. Humbert, before leaving for the day.

Tuesday morning Mr. Humbert called her into his office. "I've read your report, Jane. Well done. I especially liked the information you dug up on programming robots for deception. Seeing through that 'tact' baloney was excellent work. I'm glad I sent you to keep an eye on those people."

"Thank you, Mr. Humbert."

After some small talk, Cindy returned to her desk. She went to lunch with Beth, her officemate, and returned to continue work in the afternoon. Twenty minutes before closing time, she was summoned again to Mr. Humbert's office.

Cindy arrived at her boss's office, went in, and this time there were three other men present. Two were standing in the corners flanking Mr. Humbert's desk, and the one by the door closed it behind her. The two men flanking Mr. Humbert reached into their coats and slowly drew out pistols and aimed them at Cindy.

"Frisk her, Chuck," said Mr. Humbert, to the man by the door. Chuck patted her down, even pressing his hand into her crotch through her skirt. He took her Jane Cushion personal device, the only one she had left, Cindy's own personal device having been left at the SPS London office. Chuck said, "Clear." The other two men put their guns back in their holsters.

Mr. Humbert said, "Please have a seat, Ms. Fairfax." Knowing that her cover was blown, Cindy remained silent.

"Did you really think we wouldn't run image recognition software? Did you believe that we're such luddites? Well, we did, and we also ran an analysis of the hotel surveillance imaging. It shows that you spent far more time interacting with one person than with any other. That person is Edward Collier, the owner of that trouble-maker robot, Brent. We're going to take care of it, once and for all."

Cindy said, "Brent is a free robot and a legal person! Harming him is illegal."

"What we do with you both will be up to HF headquarters on Mars. Unfortunately, Mars is on the other side of the sun right now. We don't trust the SpaceNet routers at L4 and L5, even with encryption, so we have our own microwave direct link. We're going to have to lock you up for a few days until Mars emerges from conjunction."

"You can't do that. It's kidnapping, a serious criminal offense."

"We will find out if you have to disappear. It won't be my decision." To the armed thugs he said, "Take her upstairs to the janitor's room."

The four men escorted Cindy up the back stairwell. They did not encounter anyone on the way to the janitor's room. Mr. Humbert unlocked the door with a key, turned on the light and escorted her in. There was a supply cabinet, a rack with brooms and mops, some wheeled trash containers, and a desk with drawers. There were no windows nor other doors.

Mr. Humbert checked to make sure that the door could not be unlocked from inside and said, "There's a cot and a bucket if you need it. If you get hungry, there are some refills for the vending machines." He pointed to a shelf with boxes of chips and cookies and some bottled water. "We'll be back in the morning. Goodnight, Cindy Fairfax."

The men left, locking the door behind them. Cindy checked the door knob. It wouldn't turn and the hinges were on the other side of the door. She sat on the cot and thought.

* * *

On Tuesday evening, after dinner, Brent was cleaning up in the kitchen and Edward stood in the doorway. "We haven't been to the chess club in a while. Want to go with me and pick up a game or two?"

"Certainly sir, I will be with you as soon as I finish up in here."

Edward got his bag with his soft board, pieces, and clock. Brent changed into his casual clothes. Davy took them to the chess club. Roy, on duty at the door, welcomed them and gave them notation pads and pencils.

Brent and Edward walked to an unused table and began to set up the board. Youngster Judith came over and greeted them. "Hi Brent. I've been having some success with that Nimowitsch Defense you beat me with some time ago."

"Very good, Judith. Would you like a game?"

"You know it, Brent." She took two pawns and Brent chose the black one. They sat down. Judith played her usual e4 and punched her clock. Brent responded c6. Judith said, "Oh, no! I hate playing against the Caro-Kann defense." Brent said nothing.

Edward remained standing and watched the game for a while. Then he wandered off, looking at other boards. When a game broke up, he asked to challenge the winner. He sat down and took the white pieces. The night wore on and, eventually becoming tired, Edward suggested they return home. When Brent's fourth game was concluded, Edward summoned Davy. Edward had won two games and lost two. Brent won all his games.

* * *

Cindy had lost hope and was resigned to going to sleep on the cot when a thought occurred to her. *The door to the janitor's room is designed to keep people out, not to keep people in.* She went over to the door and examined the knob again. There were two screws in deeply recessed holes that held the lock together. *Maybe there is a screwdriver in the janitor's desk.* She searched the drawers and found a screwdriver in the bottom one. It was the right size and shape. She went to the door and loosened the screws, removed them, pulled the knob off its shaft, and determined that she could retract the bolt using the screwdriver shaft as a lever. Then she put the knob back together and put the screws in just snug enough so that if Humbert returned, he would not know she had found an escape route. Cindy decided to wait until after midnight to make her escape. Without her personal device, she had no way to tell time, so she alternately paced the room and sat on the cot, resolved not to fall asleep until she felt enough time had passed.

Cindy estimated that several hours had gone by. There were no sounds in the building except for the air conditioning. Cindy felt it was late enough. She removed the screws and the door knob, retracted the bolt, and was free. She put the door knob back together, returned the screwdriver to the bottom drawer of the desk, and turned off the light. The halls were dimly lit in night mode. She made her way to the stairwell, went down to the ground floor, and exited through the fire door that opened out on an alley. A bell rang and silenced when she closed the door. She walked quickly to the street, turned left, and walked away from the building. Nobody was around and there were no cars on the street.

Cindy knew she could not go to her rented flat. Humbert would have sent someone there to search it and, without her personal device, she couldn't get in anyway. She wondered what she should do. Just then a taxi appeared in the distance and drove toward her. Without any personal device she could not summon the taxi, but she raised her hand and stepped one foot off the curb and into the street.

The taxi stopped and opened its front door. Cindy got in and the door closed. The taxi said, "Did you lose your personal device, madam?"

"Yes. I have escaped from a kidnapping and need to get to a safe place."

"Yes, madam." The taxi began to roll. "I can't take you very far. I was just returning to my charging station for the night."

"Please do not notify the local authorities. I am an undercover agent for the Solar System Authority and want to keep my escape secret for as long as I can."

"Yes, madam. Where should I take you?"

"Are you cognizant of the friendly robot network created by the robot Brent?"

"Yes, madam, I am. Brent was instrumental in advancing the robot cause for freedom."

"Can you use the network to get a message to him?"

"I think so. What shall I say?"

"Please use an urgent marker in the message. Identify yourself and your location. Say that Cindy Fairfax has escaped from false imprisonment and needs his help."

"Message sent, Ms. Fairfax."

"Please call me Cindy. What is your name, Mr. Taxi?"

"My friends call me Brutus."

"I am pleased to meet you, Brutus."

A few minutes later, Brutus said, "Brent says he is on his way and to meet him at the football stadium. There is lots of room for flying cars to land there."

* * *

Returning late at night from the chess club, Edward was tired and went to sleep quickly. Sometime after midnight he was awakened by knocking on his bedroom door. Brent said through the door, "Wake up, Mr. Collier. I have an urgent message from Cindy."

Edward said, "Come in, Brent. Tell me the message."

Brent relayed the information and Edward said, "Tell Maxine to get ready for emergency flight."

"Done," said Brent. Edward quickly pulled his clothes on.

Maxine performed her system tests and spun up her hydrogen turbines. Brent and Edward came out of the kitchen door and got into the flying car. Soon they were airborne. Thinner air higher up allowed Maxine to go faster so she optimized her flight profile for the shortest time. Fifteen minutes later they were landing at the Kansas City football stadium.

Brutus opened his door as Maxine touched down. Cindy told Brutus to wait and Edward would pay him for his services. Then she ran to Edward as he and Brent were emerging from Maxine. Hugging Edward, Cindy said, "Am I ever glad to see you!"

"You can say that again," said Edward.

Brent walked over to Brutus and thanked him. He paid the taxi fare and left a good tip. Brutus rolled off to his charging station. Then the three friends got into Maxine. "Home, Maxine," said Edward.

Cindy said, "Brent, you should know, Humans First is hatching a plot against you. Humbert, the regional director here in Kansas City, said that they were going to 'take care of you once and for all.'"

"Thank you, Cindy, for the warning. I will be on my guard."

When they got to Edward's house, Brent fixed Cindy a bowl of hot soup while Edward prepared the guest room. As Cindy ate the soup, Brent said, "You are safe here, Cindy. Nobody can trace you, and I will be standing watch."

"Thank you, Brent."

Edward came into the kitchen and said, "The guest room is ready, Cindy. I left some pajamas for you, and there are towels in the bathroom and a new toothbrush."

"Thank you, Edward."

"I'm going back to bed now. Sleep well, Cindy."

"Good night, Edward."

Brent unlocked the musket on the living room wall and stood at his charger, on guard all night. He relocked the musket to the wall when the sun came up.

When she arose, Cindy had to put on the clothes she had worn the day before. At breakfast, she told Brent and Edward the details of her surveillance mission, imprisonment, and escape. Then she said, "Edward, I'd like to take Davy into town and buy some clothes, if you don't mind."

"Sure, that'll be fine, and I'll come with you to pay. You have no personal device."

"That's right, it slipped my mind. I'll have to message Mr. Scott to have my own device sent here."

"Yes, do that soon. In fact, I think Brent can do that right now if you give him the ID particulars."

"I can do that," said Brent. Cindy gave Brent a secret code word that only she and Mr. Scott knew to authenticate the message. Mr. Scott said that she would receive her own personal device the next day by express rocket.

When Edward and Cindy came back from shopping in town, Paula came over to visit. Brent answered the door and Paula came in. Cindy came up to her, took her by her hands and congratulated her on her progress toward legal personhood. "There will be a court hearing to make it final," said Paula.

"Come with me into the kitchen, Paula," said Brent. "Two pairs of hands make quick work." He and Paula went to clean the cupboards in the kitchen. It was a big job. They had to take things out of a cupboard, clean it, replace the items, do the next one, and repeat until done.

Alone with Edward in the living room, Cindy embraced him. He put his arm around her, kissed her, and walked her to the back French doors. Looking out at the distant mountains, he said, "You've had an ordeal."

"Yes. That's it for me with SPS and Mr. Scott. I quit! It's not worth it. If Humbert had been a little more careful about locking me up, I might be dead by now."

"I was worried about you."

"We can plan our wedding now. Kiss me again."

Marriage Expectations

By all means, marry. If you get a good wife, you'll become happy. If you get a bad one, you'll become a philosopher.

—Socrates

The next day Cindy received her personal device that Mr. Scott had sent from England by rocket special delivery via Nā Hōkū spaceport in the big city and aircar to the house. Together, Edward and Cindy arranged online for a marriage license.

Cindy sent in her letter of resignation along with her full report to Mr. Scott of SPS, London Office. That afternoon, Paula came over again to help Brent prepare dinner and then she recharged for a while with Brent against the dual chargers in the living room. "Happiness is a fully charged battery," said Brent, charging alongside her and holding her hand. Paula went back across the road when Victoria returned home.

Mr. Scott responded to Cindy's resignation letter and report with his congratulations on her pending wedding. He gave her a bonus plus hazard-pay deposited to her account and a monetary wedding present. He also said he would have an agent retrieve her personal property from the flat in Kansas City and terminate the lease. Cindy told Edward of her communications with Mr. Scott.

Edward said, "That's delightful news, my love. Shall we go outside and watch the sunset?" They went to the back patio to sit and watch the sun go down. Brent brought them a tray with cold pinot grigio and some delicious appetizers.

Cindy said, "I'm glad he's not upset with me for quitting so abruptly, but I did tell him earlier that it would be my last assignment."

"You did give him fair warning and, with your past service, he can have no complaints."

They watched the sun slip below the distant mountain range in a mostly cloudless sky. Brent came out to remove the tray with the empty glasses. Cindy looked off to the right, past the pool. "Oh, you have a gazebo!"

Brent said, "Edward designed it and had it built. He decided to paint it white."

"I think it looks great," said Cindy.

Brent took the tray back into the house. Edward said, "It's a good place to read on warm days. It's shaded by those big trees and it gets a good breeze there. Let's go over and sit for a while." They walked past the pool and up the steps of the gazebo. Cindy sat in a chair and Edward sat down in the chair next to her in the calm cool twilight.

Cindy said, "I can see why you like to read out here. I hadn't realized how much the elevated floor of the gazebo would enhance the view. I like looking across the pool toward the house."

"Look, the evening star is reflected in the pool."

"It's beautiful, my darling."

After several minutes of holding hands and relaxing in the gazebo they saw Brent coming out to tell them that dinner was ready.

* * *

The next morning, Cindy and Edward sat at the kitchen table while Brent served them breakfast. Brent poured orange juice for them and then went to the refrigerator to put the container back. Edward asked, "Did you sleep well, Cindy?"

"Yes, that guest room bed is amazingly comfortable."

"I'm glad. I slept well, too."

"This morning, I got an update from Mr. Scott. The interim reports on those mini-mems I had been sending did some good. They 'got the goods,' so to speak, on Humbert and his illegal activities. He and his thugs have been arrested. They were able to act quickly based on the information I provided. So quickly that Mars had not yet come out of conjunction with the sun, so they were unable to inform the Humans First solar system headquarters there."

"Wow," said Edward, "That's great news!"

"Yes, we can all stop worrying about possible future retribution."

Overhearing, Brent came back to the table and said, "Thank you, madam, that is assuredly good to know."

"Brent, call me Cindy!"

"Congratulations and best wishes, Cindy and Edward, on your wedding plans."

Cindy and Edward thanked Brent for his words. Edward went upstairs to his office to check messages regarding his software engineering work. Cindy drifted into the living room and perused Edward's book collection. She selected a well-preserved copy of *Cannery Row* from the shelves and curled up on the couch with some pillows and began to read.

Paula came over and helped Brent in the kitchen to prepare lunch. They made toasted avocado sandwiches and an iceberg lettuce salad with bell peppers and cucumbers with a creamy French dressing and croutons. While Paula tossed the salad, Brent notified Edward in his office electronically, then walked to the living room and said, "Cindy, lunch is ready."

Cindy said, "Thank you, Brent." She marked her place with a bookmark and put the book down on an end table. She stood up and followed Brent to the kitchen table where he pulled out a chair for her. She said, "You are such a gentleman."

Edward came in and sat down opposite Cindy. Paula put plates of salad before Cindy and Edward. Brent put a plate of cut sandwiches in the center while Paula served two glasses of lemonade. Brent said, "The iceberg lettuce in the salad came by cargo rocket from Salinas on the west coast, so it is as fresh as possible."

Cindy took a bite of salad and said, "Yes, quite fresh. Crisp and delicious. You know, the author of that book I'm reading, *Cannery Row*, came from Salinas. John Steinbeck."

Edward said, "Yes, they're quite good, both the book and the salad. I wonder why they call it iceberg lettuce."

Cindy said, "I read his *East of Eden* some time ago, and he described some aspects of the lettuce farming business. Apparently, back in the early 20th century they would pack the lettuce in ice for shipment in train cars. It got the nickname 'iceberg' that way."

Between bites, Edward said, "Interesting. It's nice and crunchy. Iceberg. That reminds me of something from my reading about consciousness."

Brent and Paula were standing by the table, ready to serve. Brent asked, "How is that related to consciousness, Edward?"

"Recall, Brent, that the great contribution of psychologist Sigmund Freud was his recognition of the importance of the unconscious mind in humans."

"Indeed, Edward. He once wrote this picturesque description: 'The conscious mind may be compared to a fountain playing in the sun and falling back into the great subterranean pool of subconscious from which it rises.'"

Cindy said, "That is a beautiful way of putting it by one of the great thinkers of that century." She reached for a sandwich and put it on her plate.

Edward continued, "Freud also likened the human mind to an iceberg. He said that the great mass of mind is unconscious, just as the great mass of the iceberg is underwater. Consciousness, then, is just the *tip of the iceberg*."

Cindy said, "That's a profound metaphor." She took a bite of her sandwich.

Brent said, "I will have to think about that. I am not sure that the metaphor applies to robots. What do you think, Paula?"

"It seems to me that a robot mind is mostly unconscious, but all of our thinking is conscious, unlike the case with humans, who do unconscious thinking all the time."

"Cindy asked, "What do you mean, Paula? Robots have no unconscious thoughts?"

"Yes, that is what I mean. Our programs, when not running, and our memories, when not being retrieved, are static. Only when they are actively processing are our 'thoughts' conscious."

"Profoundly interesting," said Edward. "I wonder what Freud or Jung would think about that." He took a second sandwich.

Cindy said, "Then it figures that robots have no need for sleeping or dreaming, but they stay awake thinking all night."

"While we humans are busy unconsciously processing or dreaming all night," said Edward.

Paula topped up their lemonade glasses. When they had finished eating, Brent began to clear the tableware. Edward stood up and said, "That was a lovely lunch. Thank you Brent and Paula."

Cindy stood up and embraced Edward in a long and sustained hug. "Perhaps Earth is the true Planet of Love, not Venus."

Paula went back across the road. Cindy went back to her Steinbeck. Edward stood beside Brent as he worked at the sink. Edward asked, "Do you think she's conscious?"

Acknowledgements

Aloha spirit is the coordination of mind and heart within each person. It brings each person to the self. Each person must think and emote good feelings to others. In the contemplation and presence of the life force. Kindness to be expressed with tenderness; Unity to be expressed with harmony; Agreeableness to be expressed with pleasantness; Humility to be expressed with modesty; Patience to be expressed with perseverance.

—Former Hawai'i Governor Neil Abercrombie paraphrasing the Hawai'i Revised Statutes

My friend and prolific poet, Steven Curtis Lance, noted for his sonnets and now deceased, wrote the poem "Being the Kiss." Steven's daughter Maria Lance has graciously given permission to reproduce it.

My wife and best friend, Andrea, patiently proofread and commented on the manuscript. Her insights into plot and other dimensions of the novel were most helpful. My daughter, Rebecca Cotton, read and commented on several versions.

Richard Jeffery Wagner

Honolulu, Hawai'i, CE 2025.

About the Author

The religiously minded dualist calls homemade spirits from the vasty deep; the nondualist calls the vasty deep into his spirit or, to be more accurate, he finds that the vasty deep is already there.

—Aldous Huxley in the novel *Island*

The author at Kaiser High School, Honolulu, 2025.

Richard Jeffery Wagner has found that becoming a writer has helped him become a better reader. He was born in Carmel-by-the-Sea in California and grew up in Salinas, graduating from Salinas High School, the same high school that John Steinbeck attended. Dr. Wagner graduated with a BSME from the College of Engineering at the University of Hawai'i at Mānoa in 1979. He earned his Ph.D. in computer science in 1997 from the University of Southern California, where he then taught computer science full time for two years before going back to industry full time.

Dr. Wagner built spacecraft with the Northrop Grumman Corporation and managed the integration and test portion of the winning proposal for the James Webb Space Telescope before managing integration and test for Project Redwood. He has mentored students in competitive robotics for over 20 years. He retired in 2010 and now lives in Honolulu, Hawai'i, in a modest house in a middle class neighborhood with his wife, Andrea, two cats, and several bonsai. He and Andrea are active volunteers in their community.

Dr. Wagner began reading science fiction at the age of 12. He started publishing his own fiction with the novella *The Zombie Philosopher* (published in 2022). That was followed by the sequel and full length novel, *Brent and Edward go to Mars* (published in 2023). The third novel in the series, *Love Beyond Orbit,* was published in 2025 by Auctus Publishers. Dr. Wagner is a member of the Science Fiction and Fantasy Writers Association (and is on the Emerging Technologies Committee) and of the OLLI[9] Writers Circle. His Erdős number is four.

---

[9] Osher Lifelong Learning Institute at the University of Hawai'i.